NEWARK PUBLIC LIBRARY-NEWARK OHIO 43055
3 2487 00311 3397

Jordan Freeman Was My Friend

Also by Richard White
in Thorndike Large Print®

Mister Grey

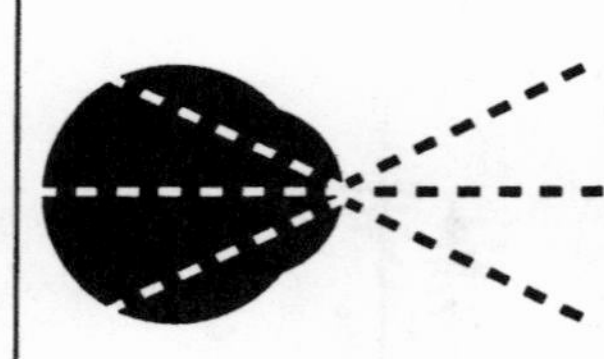

This Large Print Book carries the Seal of Approval of N.A.V.H.

Jordan Freeman Was My Friend

Richard White

Thorndike Press • Thorndike, Maine

Published in 1994 by arrangement with Four Walls Eight Windows.

Thorndike Large Print ® Americana Series.

The tree indicium is a trademark of Thorndike Press.

The text of this Large Print edition is unabridged.
Other aspects of the book may vary from the original edition.

Set in 16 pt. News Plantin by Minnie B. Raven.

Printed in the United States on acid-free, high opacity paper. ♾

Library of Congress Cataloging in Publication Data

White, Richard, 1931–
Jordan Freeman was my friend / Richard White.
p. cm.
ISBN 0-7862-0224-6 (alk. paper : lg. print)
1. United States — History — Revolution, 1775–1783 — Fiction. 2. Groton Heights, Battle of, 1781 — Fiction. 3. Afro-American men — Connecticut — Fiction. 4. Friendship — Connecticut — Fiction. 5. Freedmen — Connecticut — Fiction. 6. Large type books. I. Title.
[PS3573.H47475J67 1994b]
813′.54—dc20 94-10353

TO ALISON

with abundant and abiding love

ACKNOWLEDGMENTS

To Father Solanus Case and to other friends in high places

I am indebted beyond my powers to repay.

The people in this book — and the events of that September day — are historically true.

The only fictional character is Sally.

"Zebulon and Naphtali were a people that

jeoparded their lives unto death in the high

places of the field."

—Judges, 5:18

(inscription on the monument at Groton Heights)

CHAPTER I

I cannot stay here. The town's too full of ghosts. Squire Ledyard's offered me a berth aboard one of his ships in the West India trade, and I mean to go, to leave my father's house, my native town and all that I hold dear, perhaps never to return except in dreams. God grant my dreams are fairer then than they have been of late, or grant that I may never dream again.

Waking or sleeping, I see such things as wrench my heart and harrow my very soul. This village is haunted by the living and the dead.

Again this morning, poor crazy Azel Woodworth went past our door, hounded by a troop of thoughtless boys who pelted him with hard stones and harder names, his head lolling to one side, his eyes glazed by mingled hurt and confusion, his clothes in tatters, his gait the gait of a drunkard. Azel! He is but five or six years older than I, seven at most, but already he looks older than Moses or Elijah. Poor scarecrow. He was a youth of much promise. At sixteen, in the space of a September day, all that promise was spoiled by a musket ball that took him in the neck, scrambled his brains, and left him a poor daft derelict, the object of cold charity and scorn. It would have been better for him had he perished along with Ledyard and the rest.

Much as I mourn for all those neighbors who fell before the British and their hirelings that day, I can almost envy them their peace and their unknowing. Who can be glad to be alive in a town bereft? Who can be easy and comfortable when all around him widows, orphans, and human wreckage throng? There's little joy in it, I promise ye.

Maybe Jordan could have made some sense of it, could have found the meaning and the reason that would enable me to bide here in peace. He had a way, had Jordan, of mining out the truth of a thing and holding it up to the light so that even a fool could get at the sense of it. Jordan, Jordan, how I wish that you were here!

Jordan Freeman was my friend. I guess that he, along with Father and Colonel Ledyard, represents that ideal of manhood I have been striving toward in the years since first I met him. I was but eleven at the time. Father had some matter of business to discuss with Squire Ebenezer Ledyard, and he took me along as he often did — I being his eldest son — to

Squire Ledyard's place on Groton Heights.

It was always a delight to clamber up behind Father on the sleek brown mare, hold fast to his belt and go trotting off on whatever errand called him from our fields. That morning, as I remember, was all green-and-gold, scented with lilac and salt sea air. After a cold and rainy May, June had burst out over the land in radiant welcome warmth. On every side, bud, blossom and leaf heralded the summer's coming. Cattle waxed fat on fresh lush pasture; birds caroled from woodlot and glade; all earth swarmed with life; and the Thames, the long tidal river that divides Groton Bank from the New London shore, now yielded up a rich harvest of flounder and mackerel for idle anglers, small boys and serious fishermen.

The River Thames! How often have I paddled about on her peaceful bosom or plunged into her cooling waters to find relief from heat of summer noons. How often have I stood on her banks and observed her changing moods and colors in all seasons and all weathers. Many and many a time have I stood and watched her shipping come and go, wondering where in all the broad Atlantic the last droplets of Thames water lose their identity in the eternal great gray sea.

Soon now, I shall go down the Thames, it

may be for the last time, and sail out into Long Island Sound and beyond to the boundless sea — and whatever destiny awaits me under cloudless tropic skies. But I know that it is to this river, this harbor, this coast my thoughts will ever sail, to the very last.

Bright sparkling blue the river lay that morning, placid and fair, flowing on as it ever has and ever will, till time shall be no more. From Groton Heights, I could see the forest of masts in New London's harbor, and the houses and shops that cluster along the shore. Young as I was, I could not help feel a sense of having been blessed in just being alive and in that place upon that day.

Father, too, must have caught something of the spirit of the morning. He reined in midway between Fort Griswold and Squire Ledyard's place, and turned in the saddle to look back over the scene below.

"By God, Will, that's pretty."

Father seldom swore. And truly, the way he spoke then was hardly swearing. It was as much a prayer as anything I ever heard in church. God had made this land, and He had made that morning. So it was, in truth, pretty by God.

"I hope I am not an envious man, Will," my father went on, "but I do confess that I'd give much to have Squire Ledyard's location."

"It would be better to have his fortune," I said.

Father laughed. "Money's good, boy. I'll give you that. But the love o' money's the root of all evil, so the Scripture says. Beware of wantin' more than the Lord appoints ye."

"Does Squire Ledyard love money?"

My father shook his head. "No, Will, I don't think he does. He's a proper Christian if any man is. His wealth don't trouble him none. I guess Eben Ledyard is about the steadiest, most even-natured man in this town, even if he is the richest. I reckon he'd be the same if all his ships went to the bottom tomorrow, takin' his fortune with 'em. He's a shrewd man, but a good 'un. I never knew a better."

He took up the slack in the reins and urged the mare along. We came soon to Squire Ledyard's door, and even as I leaped down, the Squire himself came out to greet us.

"Good mornin', Captain Latham," he said. "Light and set for a bit. I'll have my gal bring us a draught of cider."

"That'd go well, Squire," said Father, swinging down from his horse. "It's middlin' warm already."

Squire Ledyard smiled. "A boon to old bones, Sir, as you will yourself discover when you are as full of years as I am."

He turned to me then and offered his hand.

"Good mornin', Billy."

" 'Mornin', Squire," said I, ducking my head.

"I declare, Captain Latham, that boy is growin' clean out of his breeches."

"He has sprouted some," said Father, ruffling my hair with his hand.

Squire Ledyard nodded. "In a few years' time, I expect, he'll be enlistin' for a soldier and marching off for a crack at the redcoats."

"God grant the war'll be over afore then," said Father.

"Amen, Neighbor," said the Squire. "There's been enough bloodshed."

"Aye." Father sniffed. "I saw enough killin' at Dorchester to last me all my days. Yet I'm fearful we shall have more of it afore we're through. What does your brother make o' those British vessels standin' off Plum Island?"

The Squire shook his head. "They trouble him, Captain Latham, they do trouble him sorely. He — ah, here comes Betts with the cider. Thankee, my gal. Captain, Will, to your health."

The cider, cool and tangy, went down most gratefully, cutting the dust of the ride. When I had drained off my mug, the Squire said to me, "Will, my nephews are over yonder in my brother's pasture admirin' the new colt. Why d'ye not run over and have a look for yourself? I know you're partial to hosses."

"May I, Father?"

"Aye. But be back within the hour, boy. There's a deal of hoein' and weedin' waitin' for ye to home."

I nodded and lit out cross-lots for Colonel William Ledyard's place. And it was there I made my mistake.

I had vaulted over the stone fence dividing the Colonel's land from the Squire's and was hipering along at a good clip when I spied something that made me pull up sharp. There on a knoll loomed a big black bull, Colonel Ledyard's Caesar, the meanest, wickedest beast on four legs.

I ought to have had more sense. Lord knows, we'd all been warned time and again to keep clear of that lot. And we all knew what Caesar was, and feared him. I can only guess that I had left my brains to home that morning; there is no other explanation.

But there I was. And it was plain that Caesar had seen me. His head was up and swinging from side to side, his eyes glittering like a toad's. He took to nodding and snorting and pawing the ground, and it was clear as if he'd written it down on paper just what his intention was. Scared? I guess. I looked about pretty briskly, I can tell ye, but that lot was well cleared. The nearest tree of any size stood a good ten or a dozen rods off, and if it came to a race between Caesar and me, well, I knew I hadn't a prayer.

Keeping one eye on the bull, I began to kind of hitch along sidewise in the direction of that tree, hoping and praying that old Caesar would take some time making up his mind. But it wasn't to be. Quick as thought, that monstrous creature put his head down and lit out after me. I didn't stay to argue. And if my feet had been equal to my intentions, no doubt I should have made that tree in two shakes of a lamb's tail. As it was, the ground stretched out before me as broad as a continent, and pelt as I might, I couldn't seem to gain any.

Caesar was gaining, though. He was digging dirt and coming on like an avalanche. The pounding of his hoofs nearly drowned out the pounding of my heart. I swear I could feel his slobber on the back of my neck, and I expected to feel something more shortly.

It being June and warmish, I had left off wearing shoes, and my poor naked feet were cut up something fierce as I nipped on over the rocky ground. My breath was whistling in my nostrils, and the sweat was streaming down my sides in rivulets. My legs were like two logs, heavy, stiff, unable to respond. I seemed to be trying to run through a pan of fudge.

I remember hearing Caesar snorting at my back, and seeing the whole landscape before me, sort of swimming in tears and sweat. And I remember thinking that it was a pretty poor way to die. I made a desperate kind of swerve to the right, hoping to dodge the ton of beef behind me, but I stepped in something unpleasant, slipped and went down hard with all the wind knocked out of me.

Caesar went thundering by like a whole battery of cannon, pulled up short, wheeled, and came charging back to finish what he'd set out to do. I hadn't time to get up on my legs again, let alone run, and I remember thinking, "Lord, prepare to receive a wretched sinner. Billy Latham's comin' home."

I shut my eyes and hoped it would be quick.

But it wasn't my time, I guess. For, on a sudden, I heard old Caesar bellow like a stuck hog, and I was sensible of a kind of scuffling, scrabbling noise, quite different from the horrid drumming that had pursued me over the pasture. I opened my eyes.

There was Caesar, kicking up his heels, bucking and flailing about like mad. And hanging on his neck, his fingers tearing at the monster's nostrils, was a giant of a man, naked but for his breeches, and black almost as Caesar himself.

What a sight that was! Bruised and shaken

as I was, I could not help but marvel at the spectacle before me. That black giant and that black bull were tearing up the pasture in the wildest, most savage kind of contest I ever hope to see. The way that bull tore was a caution, and the way that black man hung on was purely a wonder. Great chunks of turf flew in all directions, and old Caesar, for all his bulk, writhed and twisted like a serpent, blood and foam a-blowing from his nose and the sweat lathering his sides. He shook that black man the way a terrier shakes a rat, and it was plain that even so powerful a man as he could not hold on for long.

Well, I was pretty thoroughly muddled in my head by this time, but I had some sense left, and I knew I had to get help or see the black man maybe die in my stead. I got to my feet and set out on the run, hollering at the top of my voice.

Luck was with me that day. It happened that Colonel Ledyard and one of his hired men were just then coming up from the cornfield where they'd been making war on weeds. I came flying around the corner of the barn just in time to run headlong into the Colonel.

"Whoa up, there, boy!" he cried, catching me by the shoulders. "Why, it's Captain Latham's Billy! What ails you, boy? Ye look as though Satan himself was after you."

"C-Colonel," I gasped, "the bull's gone crazy. He — he's tryin' to kill a black man over to the pasture!"

The Colonel didn't linger to discuss the fine points. That wasn't his style. He and his man took off like hounds after a hare, leaving me to eat their dust all the way back to the pasture. I had no wind left, and my muscles had all turned to water. But I came along as fast's I could, and got to the stone fence in time to see the Colonel and his man drive old Caesar off with their hoes. I guess Caesar was pretty well done up, too. He made no objection, only lumbered away to sulk in the shade of that lone oak I had been so intent on reaching.

The Colonel and his hired man were bending over the black man. He lay stretched out on the ground, blood running down his face from an ugly cut on his forehead. I remember thinking, boylike, "Why, his blood's red!"

I don't know what I'd expected. I had scant acquaintance with people of color. Except for my father's servant Lambert — Lambo, we called him — I had not known any black folks up to that time. I had seen some, of course, but there's a mile of difference between seeing and knowing. And I guess I'd never given much thought to 'em. I knew they were bought and sold, like cattle, and that some people think they are descendants of Ham, the son of old man Noah in the Bible. Most men of property roundabout owned one or more blacks, and I knew that in the Southern colonies rich landowners kept whole nations of 'em to work the land for 'em. I never questioned the right or wrong of it, being but a boy and having no more care beyond fishing and fowling and such like boyish things.

But here lay a man hurt and bleeding because of me. And black or not, he could bleed, and he could feel pain. I felt pretty sick about it, though I was glad enough not to be hurt myself, and I felt a deal easier in my mind when he opened his eyes and tried to sit up.

"Easy, Jordan," Colonel Ledyard said. "Easy. Don't try to stand just yet."

The black man touched his fingers to his forehead, looked at the smear of blood on 'em, smiled a sickish sort of smile and said, "Looks like I have gone and broke my head, Mast' William."

The Colonel smiled. "You have, Jordan. I hope you've broke nothing more."

Jordan shook his head. "I reckon not, Mast' William. Seems like I'm still all of a piece."

"No thanks to Caesar, hey?" The Colonel took the handkerchief from around his neck and dabbed at Jordan's wound. "How came ye to be crossing this lot, Jordan? You know that fool bull's a four-legged demon."

"It was my fault, Colonel," said I, finding my voice at last. "I meant to take a shortcut to see the new colt. Old Caesar took out after me, and this man come a-runnin' to draw him off."

The Colonel's kind eyes widened. "So that's the way of it? Well, Jordan, it seems you are a hero today. Captain Latham will be much obliged to ye for saving this young scalawag from a trampling."

"I — I am much obliged to ye," said I, feeling my face go all hot and stupidly red.

Jordan smiled up at me. "You' welcome, Sonny," he said.

"I'm sorry you got hurt," I said. And I was, truly. It is not a pleasant thing to look down on a man that's been near killed on your account, and I was uncomfortably sensible of my fault in this.

But Jordan said, "Don't fret yourself none about Jordan, boy. I'll be right again directly."

Colonel Ledyard and his man helped Jordan to his feet; and, supporting him on either side, they walked with him back to the house. I trailed along after 'em, feeling pretty low-spirited and troubled in my mind.

The Colonel sent word to Father, over at his brother's place, and he came along promptly to see Jordan and shake his hand. He pressed some money on him, too, though Jordan was reluctant to accept it. But Father said, "Take it, man. That boy of mine is more trouble than I can well deal with, but his mother would be mighty put out with me if I was to bring him home dead or busted."

Jordan, lying on the cot in his little stone cabin, looked up at me, winked, and said, "Don't be blamin' the boy, Cap'n. Boys is all kind of chuckle-headed. It's their nature. He didn't mean no harm."

But Father did blame me. We rode home in silence, but I could hear the wheels of Judgment turning in his head. When we reined up before our door, Father waited till I slipped down, then he said, "Will, you knew better than to cross that pasture, didn't you?"

"Yes, Sir."

"And you know a man near died to save you from your own foolishness.

"Well, ye're too old for whippin' and too smart not to understand the harm you've done. Get to your chores, boy. I'll leave this day's doin's to your own conscience. Square it if you can." And he rode off at a walk to the stable.

My conscience and I put in a pretty long day.

CHAPTER II

The bright Sabbath sunlight called me early from my bed that next morning. But I was not the first to waken. Good smells of breakfast in the making wafted their way up to the garret, telling me that Mother and the gals were already up and stirring. I was known to be late for school sometimes, and even late for meeting, but I was never behind time for breakfast, nor dinner nor supper either.

I hopped out of bed, poured some water into the basin, gave my hands and face a lick and a promise, and pulled on my Sunday breeches and a clean shirt. I tugged on my stockings and wriggled into my shoes, groaning some as the cuts and bruises on my feet touched wool and leather. But it was the Sabbath, and shoes and stockings must be worn to distinguish the godly from the heathen.

Mother was just ladling out the porridge as I came into the vast kitchen. And my sisters Mary, Eunice and Lucy were bustling about laying the table, cracking eggs and tending to the sizzling sausages that snapped and sputtered on the hearth, while Luke, the baby, lay in his cradle, gumming his fingers and staring up at the whitewashed ceiling.

" 'Mornin', Will," my mother said, looking me over sharply. "You washed your hands and face?"

"Yes, Ma'am. Breakfast about ready? I could eat a hoss."

Lucy put out her tongue at me and said, "Why don't you go out to the stable then, Master Greedy?"

"Hush, Lucy," Mother said. "We'll have no quarrels on the Lord's Day."

As soon as Mother's back was turned, I pulled a face at Lucy. She made one back at me, but Mother spied her and said, "Lucy!"

"Sorry, Ma'am." Lucy hung her head and tried to look ashamed. She didn't tell that I'd made a face first. That wasn't her way. But I knew I had best be watchful for the next day or two. That girl was not one to leave an account unsettled. I could expect to find my shirttails stitched together or soap in my shoes or some such kind of mischief. I made up my mind to find me a frog come Monday. Somebody was going to be mighty startled when she turned down her sheets some night.

Father came down looking splendid in his blue coat with the brass buttons, his face all pink from shaving, and his dark hair brushed back and tied with a broad black ribbon. He was a handsome man, my father, tall and erect as befits a soldier, with a strong jaw and eyes blue as cornflowers. I have heard it said that he left a string of broken hearts behind him when he up and married Mother, and I guess it is so.

Mother herself was a beauty. I have her miniature before me as I write. Her chestnut hair, her great dark eyes, the lovely oval of her face were beyond the artist's skill to capture. But, imperfect as it is, her picture is that of an uncommonly handsome woman.

Father bid us all a good morning and took his place at the head of the table. He asked a blessing, then we all fell to with an appetite worthy of the meal. And when we'd done, Father dispatched me to the stable to tell Lambo to bring the wagon around and drive us off to meeting.

It was pleasant to go rolling through the quiet Sabbath street to the unpainted meeting house, about a mile from the ferry slip where my ancestor, Cary Latham, built the first house in this village back in 1655. (Squire Ledyard may be the richest man in Groton, but the Lathams' roots go deeper.) Folks in their best coats and bonnets were all abroad that morning, making their way to worship. Perched up on the high seat between Lambo and Father, I could not help but feel some pride at the way folks made a point of greeting Father. Looking back, I expect he was proud, too. It is no small thing to be respected by one's neighbors, and Father had earned that respect. He was one of the first men of our town to face the guns of the British Reg'lars, and he was, as captain of the battery at Fort Griswold, second only to Colonel Ledyard in bearing responsibility for the safety of the town. More than that, he was an open-handed, plain-spoken, fair-dealing man. Nobody ever got skinned in a bargain with Father, and nobody ever turned to him in time of need without receiving help and encouragement. If I can be like him, I guess I will be entitled to call myself a man.

Lambo drew up in front of the meeting house. "We're here, Cap'n," he said.

We all clambered down from the wagon and filed in to meeting. It was cool in the church, and I was glad of that. Mr. Aaron Kinne could pray longer'n any minister I ever knew, and I can't recall a Sabbath when he took less than an hour to bring the Almighty up to date on the failings and needs of us fallen mortals that dwelt on the east bank of the Thames.

And preach? My land, how that man could thunder! When he got thoroughly warmed up, he could make the windows rattle in their frames. Nobody ever slept through one of Mr.

Kinne's sermons, unless he was deaf.

This morning he took about twenty minutes to ask God's blessing on General Washington, the Congress, and the Army. He spent the next hour drawing the Lord's attention to the misdeeds of fat King George, Sir Henry Clinton, Gentleman Johnny Burgoyne, and the traitor Arnold. Arnold, of course, once lived in Norwich, a dozen miles upriver from us, so it stood to reason that he would catch it most warmly. I could hear the flames and smell the sulfur as Mr. Kinne lit into him. I would not have been from Norwich for any amount of money.

Time was when Benedict Arnold was the most admired man ever to come out of Connecticut, more so even than Governor Trumbull or poor unlucky Nathan Hale. Now I judge he is the most generally damned, and ought to be. Mr. Kinne compared him to Lucifer, the brightest of angels who became the prince of devils. I reckoned if I were Lucifer I'd have taken that unkindly.

Mr. Kinne wound down and put a lid on it. We sung a hymn, and then he took up the lesson. I scrunched down in the pew, feeling for a soft spot, but that was like looking for strawberries in January. So I just leaned back and prepared myself to endure.

Mr. Kinne took as his text, "Where are the

nine?" He told how Jesus healed ten lepers, and only one came back to say thank you. Then he tore into the subject of gratitude, and how seldom we think to return thanks for favors received.

Most times I would sit through meeting just wool-gathering and kind of dozing with my eyes open. Mr. Kinne generally talked about sins I hadn't tried yet, so I would just lay back and let the words roll over me like breakers over a stone. But this lesson hit me where I lived.

" 'Where are the nine?' " roared Mr. Kinne, slamming his hand on the pulpit with a considerable bang. "I will tell you where they are. They are howling in the Pit. Ingratitude is the worst of sins, and the ingrate is therefore the most severely punished.

"Search your hearts, I charge ye. Think whether you have left unsaid thanks to God and neighbor for benefits that you, unworthy as you are, have obtained from the bounty of Providence or from the Christian charity of some fellow creature. Thanks unspoken are a debt unpaid. And there is a debtors' prison t'other side o' the grave from which no man can be released until his accounts are settled and the last farthing has been paid.

"Ye know not when ye may be called to

your accounting, for Death cometh like a thief in the night, and no man knows when that hour will be when he must stand before the awful Judge whose eye pierces even to the most secret places of the heart and mind of carnal man.

"Pray that ye be not overtaken with your accounts unsettled, your ledgers in disarray. The way of the transgressor is indeed hard, but the way of the ungrateful is harder still."

Mr. Kinne went on to remind the congregation that he still had not received the quarter's allowance of firewood, that the roof on his house was still not repaired and last month's rains about ruined the wallpaper, that tithing was commanded by Scripture, and that the laborer is worthy of his hire.

But I was only half listening. I was thinking about Jordan. Here I was alive and in one piece because of him, and I couldn't even be certain I had said thank you. What's worse, I didn't know — and still don't know — how to properly thank a body for saving your skin at the risk of his own. But I did know if I was to die without settling accounts with Jordan, I'd go to Hell along with Arnold and the King. It wasn't a comfortable prospect.

That afternoon, as soon as I conveniently could, I slipped out from the house and looked up Lambo in the barn, where he was breaking the Sabbath by making profane music on his mouth-organ. Lambo had music in his soul. He could play more songs than I can rightly name, and he could get more music out of a Jew's harp or a comb than most people could bang out of a pianoforte. He had a fiddle he'd made himself, and folks for miles around would send for Lambo whenever there was to be any kind of charivari. Lambo had been teaching me how to play the mouth-organ. I could play *Lillbulero* and *Yankee Doodle* pretty well, and I was learning *The World Turned Upside Down.* But the fiddle was beyond me. Lambo tried, but I couldn't learn it. Scrape as I might, the only sound I got wasn't fit for Christian ears. It sounded like a sackful of cats in a hurricane.

Lambo put down his mouth-organ as I came in, and he smiled up at me and said, " 'Afternoon, Mast' Billy."

"How do, Lambo?" said I, seating myself on a nail keg opposite him.

"Pretty smart, Mast' Billy," he said, "pretty smart. You come for another fiddlin' lesson?"

"Uh-uh. I don't want to scare the cow. Besides, Father'd skin me if he caught me playin' on the Sabbath."

"Humph. Reckon he'd skin me, too. I clean forgot I ain't supposed to enjoy myself any."

"Lambo," said I, getting right to it, "what do black folks like?"

He looked at me curiously. "What do black folks like? What kind of question is that, Mast' Billy?"

"Well, I mean, if someone was to give you a present, what would you like best to get?"

Lambo grinned and shook his head. "Now who's gonna give me a present, that's what I'd like to know. And for what?"

"Drat it, Lambo, I said *if* someone was going to give you a present."

"Oh, *if*." Lambo turned up his nose and kind of snorted. "I don't need no *ifs*, Mast' Billy. That's certain. You can't spend an if; you can't eat it or drink it or make nothin' out of it. No, sir. You could have a barn full of ifs, and a cellar and a garret full, too, and you'd be no richer, nor no smarter, nor no better off than the man without a if to his name."

I could see that this kind of talk was leading me nowhere faster than I cared to go, so I laid it all out to Lambo how Jordan had saved my neck and how Mr. Kinne said I'd burn in Hell if I didn't thank him properly. "The point is, Lambo, I got to do somethin' for Jordan. And I want to give him somethin' fittin'."

Lambo frowned and looked wise. "I see how

it is," he said. "Yessir, I can see where you'd want to settle accounts. The minister has got the matter by the right handle, he surely does.

"Humph. Well, now, if it was me, and somebody wanted to thank me for somethin' — like maybe splittin' their kindlins' for 'em so their pa don't find out they neglected their chores and roast 'em, I think maybe I'd take a pouch of 'baccy or a tin of snuff and consider the slate clean."

Well, I had put my foot in it. I had been so intent on squaring accounts with Jordan that I hadn't considered what I owed Lambo. And it's true he saved me a jawing by splitting my kindlings for me only that past wash day. I was learning something. Getting rid of debts is like weeding a cornfield. You may hoe from here to breakfast, but you can never say you're done.

"Lambo," I said, "I been meaning to settle up with ye just so soon as I can lay my hands on some coins."

Lambo nodded. "Uh-huh. Well, Mast' Billy, I'll just take your meanin' and tuck it away with them ifs. When they starts takin' 'em in trade down to the store, I'll be the richest nigger in this here town."

With that, he took his mouth-organ out of his pocket and commenced to play softly. I didn't feel comfortable hanging about there in the presence of my creditor, so I said, "I better go on up to the house to see if Mother wants me for anything."

Lambo nodded. He kept on playing. He played me right out the door.

I went back to the house and trudged on up to my room in the garret. I raised a floor-board and fetched out the tin box I kept my valuables in, plopped down on the bed and took inventory. There was a willow whistle, a couple of fishhooks, a popgun and a top, an old brass key that didn't fit any lock that I knew of, two empty spools, a brass button, and not one cent. I didn't know how poor I was till I started going over the books. Not only was there no hard money, there wasn't even a thing worth trading.

I put my trash away and drifted on down-stairs and out into the sunshine, just turning the problem over and over in my mind. A debtor and a pauper at such a tender age! I would not have given the nothing I had for my prospects in this world, let alone the next. I would be lucky if I escaped the almshouse before I was a man grown.

My favorite thinking place in those days was under a pear tree in our back yard. The tree is gone now, split by lightning and converted to stove wood long ago. But sometimes, when I am troubled and beset by doubts, I go back in spirit to sit under that tree and worry things through. It helps; or seems to, which is pretty much the same thing.

I lay there that afternoon, my eyes half-closed, feeling the warmth of the earth seeping into my bones, and listening to the country sounds around me — the gentle lowing of a cow, the occasional bleating of a lamb or the bawling of a calf, the ceaseless twittering in a thousand boughs. Somewhere, far off, a dog was barking an endless muted woof-woof-woof, trying to persuade someone to come and untie him.

Maybe I dozed off. I can't be sure. But I remember sitting up with a start as a shadow fell across me where I lay, and I looked up to see Father smiling down on me.

"Snoozin', Will?" he said, seating himself beside me on the grass.

"Just thinking, Father," I said. I could see he was in his Sabbath evening mood, a mood brought on by a big dinner and a long nap.

"You seem uncommon solemn, boy. Anything troublin' ye?"

I nodded.

"Care to talk about it?"

"Father," I said, "I'm in debt."

"Ah. Well, now, that is soberin'. I have been myself in my time, Will. It cost me my sleep more'n one night. Aye, and some hours of labor, too. Ye haven't gone and taken out a mortgage, have ye? Or signed a note?"

"No, Sir. But, well, I — I feel obliged to Colonel Ledyard's Jordan."

Father nodded. "Reckon ye should, Will."

"And — and I sort of owe somethin' to Lambo, too."

"Lambo?" Father's eyes widened. "How came ye to be beholden to him?"

I laid it all out, not sparing myself any in the matter of kindlings, but trusting to Father's Sabbath mood to tide me over the rough spots.

When I'd done, Father frowned and said, "Well, you've got yourself fairly cornered, boy. That's plain."

"Yes, Sir."

Father rubbed his jaws, making a whispery sound where he'd missed some whiskers in shaving. "How d'ye propose to extricate yourself?"

I shrugged. "That's what I was sittin' here tryin' to figger out."

"And?"

I shook my head. "I've come up dry," I said.

"Well, Will, I guess I needn't stress my feelin's about your kindlin's."

"No, Father," said I, glad to see he held my low view on that particular subject.

"But there's to be no more o' that. Lambo's got his own work to do. And you have your chores, and your sisters have theirs. It's what keeps a family goin', Will, everybody pullin' his own weight."

"Yes, Sir."

"I shan't speak to Lambo about it this time. You must do that. And you must do your own work, Will. I have got to be able to rely on you, to set you a task and know that you'll do it faithful. That's as important for you as it is for me.

"When this war's over and we can pursue our affairs in peace, there'll be great chances for young men of character and grit. But character ain't a gift, Will. It's earned, day by day. I can leave you this land one day, and mebbe some stock and some hard money, but I can't give you character. I can only steer you in the way you should go, or try to. You understand that?"

"Yes, Sir."

"Humph. Well, you've had one sermon already today. I didn't mean to read ye another. But I care for ye, Will, and I mean to see you grow up straight." Father put a hand on my knee. "I'm glad you told me all o' this. I was curious to see how you'd deal with the matter o' Jordan, and I'm obliged to ye for givin' me the truth of the other thing. I'm glad to know your conscience is awake and on duty."

"It's awake, right enough. Reckon it'll keep me awake all night."

Father grinned and got up. "Well, we can't have ye losin' sleep. You've too much growin' left to do, and sleep's important. Tell me, would you like a chance to earn money to help you square accounts?"

"That's what I would like, Father," I said, getting to my feet. "But there's not many would lay out wages for a boy my size."

Father put an arm around my shoulders and started walking with me back to the house. "Tell ye what, Will. We have a sight of work goin' on up to the Fort, settin' pickets and such. If a strong boy was willin' to carry water to the men, it would save a deal of time and a lot of steps. No doubt he could make himself useful in other ways, too, runnin' errands and fetchin' tools and the like. I think Colonel Ledyard would not object to layin' out a few coppers for a steady young feller who'd mind his task and move lively."

"Could I, Father? Could I come to work at the Fort?"

"Can I rely on you not to neglect your tasks?"

"I promise, Father."

"Because I do not want to see Lambo turnin'

up at the Fort to carry the bucket in your stead."

"No, Sir. I'll do it, and faithfully."

Father nodded. "Done then." He offered his hand, and I shook it, feeling proud and suddenly much older. "School's out Saturday. You start to work next Monday mornin'."

"Thank'ee, Father," said I, feeling about as pleased as ever I'd felt in all my life before.

"Mebbe ye'll thank me again, and mebbe ye won't. 'Twon't be a picnic, Will. You must make up your mind to that I mean to work ye."

"I'll not disappoint you, Father."

"Don't," he said. Then he dug into his breeches pocket and came up with some silver. "I don't suppose that Jordan or that rascal Lambo should wait till you are solvent afore they receive their due."

He counted out four shillings into my palm and said, "That'll be deducted from your wages, Will. I trust it will serve to wipe out your debts and teach you to conduct your business more prudently hereafter."

"I will be prudent, Father, I promise." I would have promised anything, so relieved and glad was I to be thus raised up out of my difficulty.

"And, Will —"

"Yes, Father?"

"Your work at the Fort does not excuse you from your chores here, understand?"

As if he had to tell me that!

CHAPTER III

Directly after school Monday, I lit out for Mr. Chester's shop. I missed seeing a good fight, too. Ben Avery thrashed George Middleton for laughing when Ben got spelt down. George ought to have known that whatever an Avery may lack in spelling, he more than makes up for in fighting. Some knowledge comes hard.

But, sorry as I was to miss the battle, I had business that couldn't wait. I bought a tin of snuff, a pouch of 'baccy, and a stubby clay pipe. Mr. Chester warned me against falling into vicious ways, but I noticed he was willing to take my shillings anyway. I didn't bother to explain that the booty wasn't for me. It suited me to have Mr. Chester think me a boy of low character. I don't know what he thought of himself for pushing me along the road to Hell, but I hoped he'd have little joy of his profit.

I scooted along home and found Mother in the kitchen shelling peas. The gals, I knew, were still battling clothes out to the shed. Monday was a most nation tough day for them, and the smell of lye always hung about the place through Wednesday.

"Afternoon, Will," Mother said, smiling up at me. "What have ye got there?"

"Presents," said I, full of importance. "I mean to run up to Colonel Ledyard's place, Ma'am. I want to get these things to Jordan this day."

I saw no point in mentioning my gift for Lambo.

Mother nodded. "Your father said ye might be going there." She set down her collander and stood up. "I have somethin' for ye to take along."

She went over to the sideboard and fetched down a willow basket covered with a linen cloth. "Care to look?"

I raised a corner of the cloth and peered in. There was a roast fowl, some biscuits, and a pot of blackberry jam. "For Jordan?" I said.

"For Jordan." Mother smoothed down my hair and patted me on the cheek. "I'm obliged to him, too, Will. Who would split my kindlings for me if you were gone?"

Some mothers, I expect, would have carried on considerably, would have wept or gushed or fainted at having their precious boy snatched from the very jaws — or horns, I guess I should say — of Death. But that wasn't Mother's style. She was 'obliged' to Jordan. And she would have missed having me around to split kindlings. It doesn't sound like much, but it meant everything. And it was a deal less damp.

Looking back, I can't recall either Father or Mother ever saying that they loved us. They didn't have to. And besides, it wasn't their nature. Saying comes easy for some folks. But loving, well, all I know is that there was a deal of it in our house, and I am grateful.

It pleased me to have that basket, I can tell ye. The pipe and the 'baccy were good enough in their way, but they didn't seem like so much for a man that's risked his neck. Come to think of it, roast chicken and biscuits, even with blackberry jam, don't amount to a whole lot more. But I was satisfied that Jordan would know that the Lathams appreciated what he had done. That was the principal thing.

I picked up the basket and, promising to be home in time to get the chores done before supper, I slipped out the back door and traipsed on up the hill to Colonel Ledyard's.

Miss Deborah Ledyard, a saucy minx of the same age as me, was sitting on the front step working a sampler and keeping an eye on six-year-old Peter who was tumbling about on the lawn.

"Hullo, Will-yum," said Miss Deborah, pert as ye please. "I didn't know ye was comin' to call. You must excuse this old dress. I don't gen'rally receive gentlemen in anythin' so common."

"Ye needn't fret yourself," I said, with a sniff. "You don't have to wear anythin' on my account."

"Will-yum Latham!"

I don't know why it was, but ever time I talked to that gal I seemed to vex her somehow. She certainly vexed me. She had a kind of teasing way about her that made me feel more stupid than usual. And Lord knows I could do and say enough stupid things as it was, without her provoking me to more and worse.

"Really, Master Latham," said she, tossing her curls, "if my mother was to hear what you said, she'd box your ears for you."

"You know what I meant," said I, growing red in the face.

"I know what you said. And I am scandalized. Scandalized. What kind of example is that for little Peter?"

Little Peter, I might point out, was busy turning somersaults and paid no more mind to me than if I was a fence post.

"I come to see Jordan," I said, thinking it prudent to change the direction of the conversation. "Is he about?"

Miss Deborah batted her lashes at me and

said, "Oh, dear, and I had thought you'd come to call on me."

'Twasn't likely. I'd as soon have gone calling on Benedict Arnold. She knew it, too, so there wasn't any point in my saying so. But my mouth was working faster than my brains that day, and I said it.

Miss Deborah stood up and, pointing her finger at me, she cried, "Tory! Tory! Will-yum is a Tory!"

"Ye shan't say so," I cried.

"Ye said so your own self. You said ye'd like to visit Arnold. Tory, Tory, Tory!"

Je-rusalem! I wanted to kick somebody so bad it made my toes ache. Lucky for Miss Deborah, or me, or both of us, her mother came to the door about then and demanded quiet. "You stop that caterwauling, Deborah," said she. "You know your sister Sarah's lyin' sick a-bed."

That made me feel pretty cheap. I knew Sarah had been sick, and this commotion was partly of my making, though Lord knows I wanted none of it. "Ma'am," I said, feeling like Nathan Hale with the rope around his neck, "I'm mighty sorry to have disturbed Miss Sarah. I hope she may be mendin'."

Mrs. Ledyard came out onto the step. "It's you, Will," she said.

"Yes, Ma'am."

"How's your mother?"

"Pretty smart, Ma'am, thank'ee."

Mrs. Ledyard pushed back a strand of hair. "You tell her I mean to come calling soon as ever I can."

She looked terribly tired, and I felt ten times a fool for having been a party to the row. She was about to have another baby, and there was Miss Sarah lying sick within. Her little boy, Henry, had been laid to rest at the Packer's Rock burying ground only two months before, and him but a year old. She'd seen a deal of trouble, had Anna Ledyard, yet she was ever a sweet-natured woman, kind and long suffering under the weight of many trials.

She told me that Doctor Prentiss had looked in on Miss Sarah that morning, that there was no change. I said I was grieved to hear it, and I was. Miss Sarah was a handsome gal of sixteen, about the prettiest gal in the whole village, and the nicest.

I guessed that the niceness must have run out about the time Miss Deborah came along. She was sitting there pulling faces at me the whole time I was talking to her mother. I couldn't help but wish it would turn cold and freeze her like that. She could have set up in business as a scarecrow and died a rich old maid.

"What brings ye here today, Will?" asked Mrs. Ledyard.

"I come to see Jordan, Ma'am."

"Oh, yes. The Colonel told me about that. We are all very glad you wasn't trampled by that wicked Caesar."

I was pretty certain they weren't all glad, but I knew Mrs. Ledyard was, and I thanked her politely.

"Jordan's restin' in his cabin out back, I believe. The Colonel said he wasn't to work until he was feelin' fit again."

"I'll just go 'round, then, and look in on him."

"You do that, Will. And be sure to greet your mother for me."

Mrs. Ledyard went back into the house, and as I turned to go around back, that Miss Deborah called softly, "Will-yum?"

I turned back. She sat there looking as if butter wouldn't melt in her mouth. "Will-yum, you are an uncommonly nice looking boy," she said, catching me altogether off stride. Then she added, "For a damned Tory."

If she'd have been a boy, I'd have thumped her till she hollered. As it was, there was nothing I could do but wrap myself in my dignity and stalk off to see Jordan. But my ears were red, and I knew it. It is hard to be dignified with red ears.

The door of Jordan's cabin was ajar to catch the breeze blowing in off the river. I rapped my knuckles smartly on the panel, and I heard a voice call out, "Who's there?"

I stuck my head in and said, "It's me, Jordan. Billy Latham."

"Come in, boy. Come in and set."

It was dim and cool inside the cabin, and my eyes were slow to adjust to the change from the bright sunshine outside. I half-stumbled, half-groped my way in, bumped into a table and set my basket down on it. I blinked a few times, squinted, and began to make out my surroundings.

There wasn't what ye'd call an abundance of furniture. There was the table, two ordinary sort of chairs such as ye might find in any attic, a washstand with a pitcher and basin, a cracked looking-glass, some shelves with a dish or two and a tin cup, and against the far wall a cot, on which Jordan himself was sitting.

"How do, Jordan?" said I, peering hard at him in the faint light.

"Tolerable, boy. Tolerable. Take a chair. I ain't had no company all day, and I was beginnin' to feel myself neglected."

I dragged a chair up close to Jordan's cot and sat down. "I'd a-come sooner," I said, "but, well, I had some things to do."

Jordan nodded. "Glad you come a-tall."

My eyes were getting accustomed to the light, and I could make out his face pretty distinctly. He was very black, was Jordan, and the white bandage around his head made a sharp contrast with the color of his skin. He'd a white shirt on, too, and it helped me to make him out more plainly.

"Jordan," said I, "I came to thank ye for what ye done."

"No need to, boy," he said.

"Well, but, it was my fault you got hurt, and — well, I'm ashamed and sorry and thankful, too." It was a lot to say, and it cost me something to say it.

Jordan must have sensed that. He gave a low whistle, and he chuckled softly. "My land, boy. You been practicin' to say all that?"

I was glad it was dim, because I could feel myself getting red. It was true. I had rehearsed what I meant to say, and I had to say it quick or I'd never have said it all. "It's been on my mind to say it," I allowed.

"Well, now, I'm glad your mind's unloaded. Now we can just neighbor easy."

"I-I brought ye somethin', Jordan," I said.

"Did ye now?" Hum. Well, it wasn't looked for, but it's welcome."

I got up and dug the pipe and the 'baccy

out of the basket. "Here," I said. "This is for you."

"Say, now! Looky here. A pipe and tobacco. I call that handsome. I surely do." He made a great show of examining the pipe and sniffing the 'baccy. "That's quality goods, boy, store-bought and prime. Your pa must have tapped his strong box for these articles."

"I bought 'em myself," I said, "with my own money."

"Did you?" Jordan looked impressed. "Now that is handsome. Lots of boys would have just wheedled the money out of their pa, but you know how to do a thing right. Shake hands, boy. I admire your style."

Jordan's big hand enveloped mine in a firm grip. "A boy like you is worth a busted head to save."

"Does it hurt much?"

"Naw. It was buzzin' some this mornin'. I thought mebbe I'd swallered a bee in my sleep. But I expect I'll be up and stirrin' good as new tomorrow."

"I'm glad," I said. There was an awkward spell of silence. Then I said, "Oh, Mother sent ye that basket."

"Did she? I see that basket when you come in, but I didn't want to get my hopes up too high. I already got a bran' new pipe, and tobacco to smoke in it. But a basket, too! Um-

umph. Reckon I ought to go into the business of savin' Lathams. 'Pears to me there'd be a fortune in it."

I had to laugh. Then I said, "You want to know what she fixed you?"

"I guess," said Jordan, getting up from his cot and moving to the table. He just about filled that cabin. I hadn't realized how huge a man he was. I could see now how he had dared to tackle old Caesar.

"Biscuits!" he cried. "And a whole roast chicken! And what's this? What's this?"

"Blackberry jam," I said.

"Blackberry." Jordan sort of sighed the word. "Blackberry jam. If they is a thing I'm partial to in this whole world, it is biscuits with blackberry jam. You tell your ma that Jordan said he is much obliged. Very much obliged."

"She said she's obliged to you."

"No."

"Yes. She said if anythin' had happened to me, she wouldn't have nobody to split her kindlings for her."

"Ha-ha-ha!" The laughter rumbled up from deep in Jordan's chest. "Think of a mother sayin' that! Ha-ha-ha!"

"What's all the merriment?" cried a stern voice from the doorway, making me jump near out of my skin.

"Why, Mast' William," said Jordan, ducking his head, "you come to look in on Jordan, too?"

"I have," said Colonel Ledyard, stepping into the room. "But I see you have company."

"My friend Billy Latham dropped by. But come in, Mast' William, do. Billy fetch a chair for the Colonel."

"How are ye, Will?" said the Colonel.

"Pretty smart, Colonel," said I. "I trust ye're keepin' well."

"Very well, thank'ee. Jordan, how are you feeling?"

"Better by the minute, Mast' William. Reckon I'll be fit for work in the mornin'."

"Well," said the Colonel, seating himself on the chair I'd brought for him, "that's as may be. But what's all this plunder, hey?"

"That? Why, that's a basket sent by Miz Latham by way of sayin' thank'ee for splittin' her kindlin's."

Well, that got me to laughing, and Jordan had to explain, and then the Colonel had to laugh, too. "I knew your mother when she was Eunice Forsyth, Will," he said. "All the Forsyths were known for their humor. I am glad to know your mother has not lost her share of it.

" 'Twas thoughtful of her to send along that basket, wouldn't ye say so, Jordan?"

"Mighty thoughtful, Mast' William. And when it comes to bein' thoughtful, this boy here don't take a back pew to nobody. Looky here, Mast' William. Did y'ever see a finer pipe?"

Colonel Ledyard took the pipe in his hands and studied it closely. "No," he said, at last, "I never saw a finer."

"Billy gave me that. And tobacco."

"And tobacco?" The Colonel shook his head. "Jordan, they are out to spoil you."

"So I believe, Mast' William," said Jordan, laughing. "I don't see how I'll be able to go back to ploughin' after today. I feel 'most as rich as the Squire hisself."

"Hum," said the Colonel, passing his hand over his mouth. "Now I am perplexed."

"How so, Mast' William?"

"Well, ye see, Jordan, I came here on purpose to make you a present myself."

"Lord A'mighty," said Jordan, throwing his hands up in the air. "More presents!"

"Ay-uh." The Colonel sniffed. "Thing is, Jordan, I think a good deal of my neighbor Latham. And I know he sets considerable store by this boy of his. Besides, not to make a speech about it, I think you did a handsome thing over there in the pasture. Very handsome.

"But," said the Colonel, "I haven't brought

you a pipe, or tobacco, or a basket. And maybe my gift won't look like so much alongside all that. The Lathams have put me in the shade, and no mistake."

"Mast' William," said Jordan, "I didn't look for no presents. Indeed I did not."

"I know it, Jordan." The Colonel got to his feet. "But they're comin' to ye all the same."

He offered his hand to Jordan, and Jordan, looking some bewildered, took it. "Jordan," said the Colonel, "as of this day, ye're a free man. I'll make out the papers this evening, and with tomorrow's sunrise you're at liberty to go."

Jordan's jaw dropped. "Free, Mast' William?"

"Ay-uh. That's my present to ye. Ye can't smoke it and you can't eat it, but it may do ye more good in the long run. I surely hope so."

"God A'mighty! Great God A'mighty!" Jordan sat down on the bed and buried his face in his hands.

Colonel Ledyard placed a hand on Jordan's shoulder. "Ye've been a good and faithful servant, Jordan, as it says in the Scripture. I'll give ye a good character and sign it myself. It should help you to find work wherever ye choose to go."

Jordan raised his face to the Colonel, and

I marveled to see traces of tears on those black cheeks. "Go, Mast' Will — Colonel? Where should I go?"

"Why, anywhere ye've a mind to. You are free, and free to choose."

Jordan wiped his nose on his sleeve and rubbed at his eyes with the heels of his hands. He shook his head, swallowed hard, and said, "Colonel, I — I am more obliged to you than I can rightly say. Bein' free — well, I have dreamed of it. I surely have. But I never wished to go away from here. You and Miz Ledyard have been more'n good to me, when you had title to use me like a hoss or an ox or any other creetur belongin' to the place. You allus treated me like a man, Colonel, which is what I am. And I am purely grateful."

Colonel Ledyard tugged at his long straight nose, then he said, "I am glad you feel we've dealt fairly with ye, Jordan. But the truth of it is, when a whole nation's roused to fight for freedom, and I am myself pledged to fight — and die, if need be — for freedom, it's a contradiction for me to keep a fellow creature in bondage. It just doesn't square somehow, and I had meant for you to have your liberty in any case. This business with old Caesar only served to remind me of what I meant to do, and ought to have done long ago."

Jordan stood up, towering over even the Colonel. "I take your gift, Colonel, and I thank you."

"You are welcome, Jordan, though I'm not certain your freedom is mine to give ye." Colonel Ledyard smiled up at the young black giant. "I feel I am still in your debt, and I'd take it kindly if ye'd name a way for me to settle it."

Jordan's own smile was beautiful to see. "Hire me," he said. "I know this place; I know what needs doin'. One way or another, ye'd have to replace me. And a new man would have to learn it all from scratch."

Ledyard grinned. "Done!" said he, offering his hand. "We'll argue about your wages in the morning. Get your rest now, my friend. You start a new life tomorrow. Jordan the slave doesn't live here anymore. I have hired Jordan the free man."

The Colonel left then, and Jordan began to caper about the little one-room cabin like a man that's stepped on broken glass. "A free man! You heard the Colonel, boy. I'm a free man now. Whoop! Free and earnin' wages! Ha-ha! Free and earnin wages! Praise the Lord, boy! Praise the Lord!"

When his first fit of jubilation had passed, Jordan tried to sit. But he couldn't seem to stay put. He was just boiling over with gladness, and it did me good just to look at him.

"Goin' to save up money, boy," he said. "Goin' to lay my money by. I have got a use for it, I surely have. And when I've done that, why, I mean to lay up more. Someday mebbe I'll buy me a little farm and set up for a man of property. I'll call myself Mister Jordan Freeman, 'cause that's what I am. A free man. And I'll have me a cow and mebbe a hoss, and I'll ride around this here town same as any other free man."

"That'll be fine, Jordan," said I, feeling a little awed and a little nervous for fear the excitement might bring on a fever. "That'll be fine."

"Fine? I guess." Suddenly Jordan picked me up clean off the floor and near hugged the life out of me. "It's your doin', boy. It's all your doin'. If you hadn't agone crosslots and stirred up old Caesar, I might have lived and died a slave."

"B-but the Colonel said he was a-goin' to s-set ye free, Jordan."

"Mebbe he was, and mebbe he wasn't. But he done it. And he done it because of you. Whoop! Oh, Billy Latham, you surely are a friend worth keepin'."

He set me down then, and I counted my ribs to see if he'd broke any. He hadn't. But I was sore for a week after.

"Well, Jordan," I said, "I have got to get along home."

"Come see me, boy. Don't you be a stranger, now."

I promised I'd come, and I said, "Jordan, I'm awful glad."

Jordan's smile would have made a sick man well just to see it. "Me, too, Billy. Me, too. God A'mighty, but it surely feels good. I feel good all over."

I nodded and started for the door.

"Hey, Billy?"

"Yes?"

"You know the first thing, the very first thing I mean to do as a free man?"

"What, Jordan?"

"I mean to take up smokin'."

CHAPTER IV

Fort Griswold, named for The Honorable Matthew Griswold, Esquire, deputy-governor of the State of Connecticut, was Colonel Ledyard's pride. The Fort had been his special care since its construction was ordered back in '75. On July 3rd, 1776, he was appointed captain of the artillery company and commander of the Fort. Two years later, his command was enlarged to take in Stonington to the east and New London to the west. He was then promoted to the rank of major, with responsibility for shore batteries in Stonington, and Fort Trumbull and Fort Nonsense across the Thames. Father, who had been a lieutenant in the battle of Dorchester Heights, was made captain and put in command of Fort Griswold under Ledyard.

Father used to grumble sometimes that the Colonel would do better to spend more time in New London and leave the managing of Fort Griswold to him. But Fort Trumbull was hardly more than a block of batteries facing the river's mouth, and Fort Nonsense was a mere breastwork of heaped up earth on Town

Hill, boasting but six or eight guns. With the scarcity of arms and materials, there was no hope of strengthening either of these posts, so Fort Griswold was the principal defense of the region and Ledyard, who had all but built it himself, gave it nearly all of his time and care.

Unlike Nonsense and Trumbull, Griswold was a real fort, covering more than an acre of ground on the Heights overlooking the harbor. There were barracks and a magazine, a parade ground and a triangular breastwork to protect the gate near the flagstaff in the southwest bastion. The walls were of stone, rising some ten or twelve feet in height, and above the west wall, facing the river, was a platform for cannon, and a parapet which a man might shoot over by mounting a step. There was a battery of cannon east of the Fort, and another below the western wall, its guns trained on the opposite shore.

That summer of '81, the men were kept busy setting inclined pickets in place all along the rampart as a further discouragement to any invader who might be fool enough to storm the Fort. And my task, once school was out, was to fetch and carry water for the sweating soldiers.

I must have traipsed above a hundred miles, just lugging buckets to and from the well. I think I lengthened my arms a good three inches in the course of my labors. I worked. Indeed, I never worked so hard or so steadily in all my life before. But it was work I thoroughly enjoyed. I learned more about drilling, cussing and other soldierly pursuits than was perhaps fitting for a boy of my years. But there are times when knowledge of that kind has its uses, and I was glad of the chance to acquire it.

There were, at any given time, about 150 men assigned to the Fort. These were militia, not Continental Army men; although some, like Father, had seen Army service. Just about every able-bodied man in the surrounding countryside did a stint of soldiering at one time or another. And all were expected to come a-running if the alarm sounded. With any kind of notice, Ledyard should have been able to muster upwards of 600 men.

The militia didn't have uniforms as such, and their weapons were about as varied as their dress. A few, very few, had good Pennsylvania pieces, so accurate that a man could pick a flea off a dog's ear at a hundred paces. Most had muskets or fowling pieces of indifferent quality, and some had only spears or pikes. Our trust was in our cannons. An attack, if it came, would come by water. And those big guns could lob an 18-pound ball upwards of a mile. Lord, how I wished I could touch one off! You could make a mighty noise with one of those, I promise ye. But, although the men drilled daily in loading and sighting those big thunderers, they did no actual shooting. Powder and shot were too precious to spend in mere practice.

The work of setting the pickets went along pretty smartly during that last week in June, and I was kept so mortal busy that I had no time to go swimming or fishing or to do any of those things summer was created for. I did not think myself ill-used. Indeed, I counted myself the luckiest boy in the whole town. But generally, once supper was done, I had only about enough strength left to drag my carcass up to my bed, where I'd lie like a corpse until morning.

I kept meaning to go up to Colonel Ledyard's place to look in on Jordan, but the days kept sliding by, and I was just too tuckered evenings. Then, on a sultry afternoon about the first day of July, Tom Avery, a great fellow of seventeen or so, son of Lieutenant Parke Avery, came up to me as I was straining to haul up yet another bucket from the cool depths of the well.

"Billy," he said, "your pa wants ye."

I hadn't heard him come up, and when he spoke it gave me such a start that I let go the rope, and the dratted bucket went plummeting all the way back down again. "Jerusalem, Tom!" I said. "Ye scairt me out of a year's growth."

Tom just laughed and said, "Come along lively."

I fell in step with him, and we headed for the magazine, where Father was standing deep in talk with Colonel Ledyard.

"Here's Billy, Cap'n," Tom said.

"Oh, Will. Looky here. We just learned that Colonel Harris is coming over from New London this afternoon with a wagonload of powder. I gave some of the men liberty to go cool off with a swim, so we are a mite shy on muscle. We want ye to run over to the Colonel's house, find Jordan, and tell him there's a chance to pick up some hard cash here if he's of a mind to stretch himself."

"Very well, Father," I said, glad of the excuse to leave off toting buckets, and gladder still at the prospect of seeing Jordan again.

"Oh, and if you can find Lambo, tell him to stir himself and get right on over here. We are sure to get a shower this evenin', and I want that powder in afore the rain starts."

I nodded and took off on the run. But that run soon slowed to a pretty lame trot, so hot and breathless was the day. I hadn't far to go, but going at all was mighty strenuous.

Mrs. Ledyard, looking wan and peaked, was sitting on the front step trying to stir up a breath of air with a palm-leaf fan. From the look of her, it wasn't doing much good.

"How do, Mrs. Ledyard," said I. "Is Jordan anywhere about?"

"No, Will. I sent him to fetch Dr. Prentiss. Poor Sarah is suffering so with this heat and all. She is low, poor darling, very low."

"I'm awful sorry, Ma'am. We should get a shower this evenin'. That'll cool things off some."

"Lord, I hope so." Mrs. Ledyard sighed. "This weather's hard enough on a well person, let alone a sick one."

"Yes, Ma'am." I felt awkward standing there, trying not to appear to notice how big Mrs. Ledyard was getting with her baby, and trying to think of something cheerful to say to a lady that needed cheering about as bad as a fish needs water.

"Jordan will be back directly, Will," Mrs. Ledyard said. "Would ye like to step inside and wait?"

Well, I didn't want to. And I'm ashamed to say why. But the truth is, I was afraid of coming down with whatever it was ailed Miss Sarah. I was none too comfortable around sick people anyway, and I was not much better around folks as troubled as Mrs. Ledyard was.

So I said, "If ye think it'll be all right, Ma'am, I will just go around back to Jordan's cabin and wait for him there. My — my feet are awful dusty, and I don't want to track up your house."

"That will be all right then," said Mrs. Ledyard, her voice faint and dreamy like. She was looking at me, but I wouldn't swear that she was seeing me. It was as if I wasn't there anymore.

"Ma'am?"

"Yes? Oh, Will. I guess I was wool-gathering."

"Yes, Ma'am. I — uh, I will just go around back and wait for Jordan. You'll tell him, won't ye? He's wanted at the Fort."

"Yes, Will. I'll tell him."

I slipped off to Jordan's cabin, glad not to have to talk anymore. I liked Mrs. Ledyard. I really did. She was a pleasant woman, and a good one. But it gave me the whim-whams to stand there and try to make talk with a body that seemed to look right through me.

Jordan's door had no lock, so I just let myself in, grateful for the dank coolness that no amount of July sun could ever drive out. I was almighty hot and tired, and kind of headachey from so much scurrying around in the open, so I sat down on Jordan's cot and rested. Maybe I dozed off; I disremember. But all of a sudden I was conscious of a slight sound. I started up and saw a broad figure filling the doorway.

"What you doin' here, boy?"

It wasn't Jordan. The man stepped into the room, and as he crossed before the one small window, the light slanted in on him. As it did so, my bowels knotted up like a kite string. A blind man could see that here was a sure enough Injun.

I admit I was scared. I never had much dealings with Injuns, but I had heard such stories from my grandfather about the French War as to make me sweat whenever I passed one on the street. There were still a fair number of 'em about, Mohegans mostly, and some Pequots. But they were all pretty tame, really, taking work when they could find it, charity when they had to, and living hard mean lives on the edge of the white man's towns. Looking back, I can see now that I had no call to be afraid, but I was all the same.

"What you doin' here?" the red man said again.

"W-waitin' for Jordan," I stammered. "But I guess he ain't c-coming."

The man let his dark eyes travel slowly around the room, then they lit on me and held there. "You touch anything?"

"N-no. No, I didn't. Jordan's a friend of

mine. I wouldn't touch his stuff."

The Injun folded his arms on his broad chest. "Mebbe not."

"I tell ye I didn't," I said, my voice shaking as bad as my knees. "I'm goin' along now. I can't wait. You tell Jordan —"

"You stay. Wait for Jordan."

"I can't," said I, making for the door. I got past the man, meaning to make tracks, but it wasn't to be. His hand shot out and nabbed me by the nape of the neck. I felt my feet come off the floor, and before I could so much as squeak, that Injun lugged me over to the bed and slung me across it. Then he very calmly sat down on top of me, saying, "You stay. Wait for Jordan."

I was never in such a fix in all my life. Plain sense told me there was no use in struggling. But my bones told me that if Jordan didn't show up pretty quick, I would be mashed flatter than a flapjack. There are more comfortable situations, I promise ye. I told myself I'd be cussed if I'd cry, but I surely felt like crying. And I probably would have, too; but, fortunately, Jordan turned up.

He stuck his head in the door and said, "Billy?"

"Jordan!" I gasped. "Save me!"

Jordan stepped in, took one look, and set to laughing so hard he liked to have died. He cackled and roared so that he had to lean against the wall to hold himself up. "Ha-ha-hah! Oh! Whew! Ah-ha-hah-hah! B-Billy, ye're ketched!" he cried. "Hold on to your hair, boy. Ha-ha-hah!"

I confess I missed the humor of it. "Make him get off, Jordan. Please! I'm smotherin'."

"Ease up, Tom," Jordan said, wiping his eyes. "That there's a friend of mine, Billy Latham. It was him brought that chicken you helped me polish off t'other day."

A great weight was lifted from my suffering bones, and I heard the Injun say, "This the boy the bull was after?"

"That's him, Tom. And I would take it kindly if you would not use him so hereafter. I got — ha-ha-hah — I got chairs enough for everybody."

The Injun turned to me, unsmiling. "Sorry, Billy Latham," he said. "I thought mebbe you come to steal from Jordan."

"Shake hands with Tom Wansuc, boy," Jordan said. "Tom's a good friend o' mine. He'll be your friend, too, if you can forgive him."

Well, I wasn't sure I wanted to be friends with a man who had just about squashed the life out of me, but I judged it wouldn't be convenient to have him for an enemy, either. Besides, he was a friend of Jordan's. I stuck out my paw.

"We're friends now," Tom Wansuc said, pumping my arm two or three times. "You come fishin' now with me and Jordan. Catch eels for supper."

In those days, I'd sooner go a-fishing than most anything, but I explained that Jordan and I were needed at the Fort.

"What for?" Jordan asked.

"We're gettin' in a load of powder," I said, "and Father needs extra hands to unload it. He says there's hard money in it for you."

"Well, now, I got a use for that," said Jordan, grinning. "You come, too, Tom. We'll work this afternoon and go fishin' this evenin'."

Tom Wansuc nodded. "Could use some money," he said. "Let's go."

I left them and went on down to my house to rouse Lambo. By the time he and I got to the Fort, the wagon was just pulling in through the gate. Colonel Harris, a puffy old body rigged out in a sky-blue broadcloth coat despite the day's heat, reined in beside the wagon and got stiffly down from his big bay horse. Father and the Colonel came up to greet him.

"Good day, Colonel. 'Day, Captain," Harris said, doffing his tricorn hat and mopping his face with his handkerchief. "Here's your powder, come down from Lebanon this morning."

"And very welcome it is, Colonel," said Ledyard. "I'll set the men to unloading directly."

"Good, good," said Harris, looking anxiously up at the gathering clouds. "I would like to get home before the rain comes. Don't want to spoil my coat."

I saw Father wink at Colonel Ledyard, but Ledyard pretended not to see. "Let us go over and stand in the shade, Colonel," he said, "I want to discuss some matters with ye while the men unload."

In no time at all, the men were lined up between the wagon and the powder-house, and they started passing the kegs from hand to hand. Tom Wansuc and Jordan shucked off their shirts and pitched in with a will. And I was told off to fill my buckets and stand by to ladle out water to the toiling men.

"You might bring a bucket over to us, too, Will," Father said. "I'm sure Colonel Harris would be grateful of a drink."

I hauled up a bucket, all cold and dripping, and lugged it across the parade ground to where Harris, Ledyard and my father stood. I set my burden down and offered a brimming dipper to Colonel Harris.

"Thank'ee, my lad," said Harris, patting me on the head. Ugh. I hated being patted on the head. But grownup folks will do that. Maybe it makes 'em feel big, I don't know. But if I should ever marry and have children, I hope I will have sense enough not to do that.

Harris drained off the dipper, making more noise than a horse at a trough. "Hah!" he said, wiping his mouth on the back of his hand. "Gad, Sir, that's good. Riding's monstrous dry work on such a day as this. Have a drink, Colonel?"

Ledyard shook his head.

"Captain?"

"No, thank'ee, Sir," Father said. I guess I wouldn't have cared to drink after Harris myself, the way he about swallowed the whole dipper.

Harris's little eyes wandered over to the wagon. "By Gad!" said he. "Whose nigger is that? The big fellow, I mean, nearest the wagon."

"He is nobody's nigger," replied Ledyard. "He works for me. His name is Jordan Freeman."

"Why, he is a black Hercules. Look at those shoulders! I'll wager he could lift an anvil over his head without working up a sweat." Harris frowned. "I've seen him somewhere before, I think. Odd. I can't seem to recall where."

He shook his head, making his jowls wobble. "Well, no matter. But what a splendid animal he is. And that Injun working alongside him! By Jupiter, he may not be so tall as the nigger, but will ye look at the muscle on that heathen! Wouldn't I love to see those two mix it in a fight!

"You, boy."

"Yes, Sir?"

"Run along over there and tell those two to step this way."

I glanced up at Father. He nodded, and I trotted off. "Jordan," said I, as I came up to the wagon, "Colonel Harris wants to talk to you and Tom Wansuc."

"Does he?" said Jordan, not pausing in his labors. "Well, Tom, reckon we better go over and see what he wants."

"Guess so," said Tom, passing along a keg to Luke Perkins.

Together, Tom and Jordan followed me over to the clump of trees where Colonel Harris stood with Father and Colonel Ledyard.

"You wanted to see us, Colonel?" Jordan said.

"I did," said the New Londoner, rocking back and forth on his heels. "How would you two like to earn a gold piece?"

Jordan and Tom exchanged glances. "I guess we'd have no objection to that," Jordan allowed. "What do we have to do?"

"Well," said Harris, smoothing his white waistcoat over his paunch, "it's this way. I am giving an entertainment for some important friends from Hartford. And I thought it might amuse 'em if you and this Injun was to stage a wrestling match for 'em."

Jordan looked at Tom Wansuc. Tom looked back blankly at Jordan, not so much as a flicker of expression in his eyes. Then Jordan said, "Well, Colonel, I guess not."

"You guess not?" Harris's eyebrows shot up. "I'm talking about a Spanish gold piece, man. And five of 'em to the winner."

"Guess we better get back to unloadin', Tom," Jordan said. He turned to go.

"You, Injun," said Colonel Harris, "think o' the rum ye could buy with a piece of Spanish gold."

Tom Wansuc grunted. "Can't wrassle all by myself," he said. "And it don't look like Jordan's of a mind to."

"Talk to him, then. No nigger's so prosperous that he can turn up his nose at a gold piece. You persuade him, and I'll throw in a quart of my best Jamaica rum for ye."

Tom Wansuc didn't bat an eye. "I'm partial to sarsaparilla myself," he said.

Harris turned to Colonel Ledyard. "Talk to your man, Colonel," he said. "Make him see he's acting like a fool."

A faint smile played about Ledyard's mouth. "Thing is, Colonel, Jordan's his own man. If he chooses not to wrestle, there's not a blessed thing I can do about it."

"Damnation!" Harris puffed and blew like a grampus. "Ye'd think even a nigger'd have more sense."

He glared at Jordan. "You ain't afraid of this Injun, are ye, a big fellow like you?"

Jordan nodded. "That's it, Colonel," he said. "Tom's a Pequot. Fullblooded. If I was to get him riled up, there's no tellin' how bad he might hurt me. Even a Spanish gold piece ain't goin' to buy me new hair."

Father made a funny choking kind of sound and seemed to find something mighty interesting going on up in the branches of the trees.

"You're afraid of getting hurt?"

"Yessir," Jordan said.

"Well! Well!" Colonel Harris fumed and sputtered. "If I hadn't any more gumption than that — !"

"You can wrestle Tom if ye've a mind to, Colonel," Jordan said. "Me, I got a wagon to unload."

And he walked off just as calm as ye please.

Tom Wansuc, his face sober and dead serious, said, "You want to wrassle me, Colonel?"

"Damn your impudence!" cried the Colonel. "Get back to your work before I take my stick to you."

Tom's hand darted out like a snake and caught up the colonel's silvermounted cane. "Pretty stout stick," he muttered. And he snapped it in two with a crack like a musket shot, and dropped the pieces at the outraged Colonel's feet.

I thought Harris was about to burst. His face went red as a turkey's and he shook like a leaf in a gale. I was scared, I can tell you. But Tom Wansuc only eyed the Colonel up and down, then gave a hitch to his breeches and went back to help Jordan with the work.

As for me, I suddenly remembered I had business over at the well.

CHAPTER V

Father told me later that Colonel Harris was for having Tom Wansuc jailed, hanged and horsewhipped, not necessarily in that order. But there didn't appear to be any volunteers for the job, so the old fellow had to content himself with a deal of cussing and considerable big talk about how he'd have that heathen in irons if he was in command of Fort Griswold. I noticed, though, that he slunk off pretty meek when the work was done. He didn't stay around to neighbor any.

My opinion of Tom had improved considerably since that morning. I confess, I did not like being sat on, and was of a mind to resent it. But seeing Tom stand up to Harris like that was another matter. That took some grit, and I was not too young to appreciate that.

I was troubled about Jordan, though. I couldn't see why he had refused to wrestle Tom. And I had to allow that Colonel Harris had a telling argument about the gold piece. Shucks, I guess I'd have wrestled Tom myself for that, and taken the money along with the licking, and smiled.

Was Jordan afraid of Tom? I couldn't credit that. A man who'd tackle a bull wouldn't shy off from tackling another man, not even so strong a man as Tom Wansuc. It didn't make sense. And it made me uncomfortable in my mind. I did not want to think Jordan a coward. But he said his own self that he was afraid to lock horns with a Pequot. It set me to wondering, I admit, and I didn't like to have to wonder. It seemed to me then that a person ought always to act in such a way so as to leave no doubts in another's mind. I reasoned that knowing a person meant knowing how he would act in any circumstance. And I surely never expected that Jordan would back away from a fight.

Well, it troubled me. But I kept my trouble to myself for the time being, meaning to get at the root of it at the first opportunity.

That opportunity came in the wake of the biggest news to hit these parts since Arnold turned his coat. It was a week or so after Harris's visit to Fort Griswold when Sergeant Stephen Hempstead rowed from Fort Trumbull to report the taking of the British merchant ship *Hannah* by Captain Dudley Saltonstall of New London.

I guess that when the scholars sit down to write the history of those times, they will spill a lot of ink on the Saltonstalls. The father,

Gordon, was serving as a brigadier in the very first year of the war. His son Winthrop, the eldest, worked in the admiralty office; Gilbert, the youngest, was a captain of marines; and this Dudley ended up a commodore before the shooting stopped.

On that particular day, however, Dudley Saltonstall was cruising around Long Island in his privateer, *Minerva*, when he intercepted the *Hannah* on her way from London to New York. It was a handsome prize; indeed, her cargo later proved to be the richest taken in the whole course of the war. And that is saying something, when ye consider how busy the privateers were in those times.

Well, the whole region was agog with excitement and curiosity. Folks flocked to New London from miles around to see the *Hannah* and to gloat over all those provisions that would never reach Sir Henry Clinton and his forces in New York. Dudley Saltonstall was the hero of the hour, and there was an air of general rejoicing at the neatness of the thing.

Of course I had to go to see the *Hannah* for myself. Father was against it. "You'll get yourself trampled in the crush, Will. I know it."

But I protested that I had more sense than that, that I could get out of the way as nimbly as the next fellow, that it was hard, when all the world was turning out to view the prize, that I should have to content myself with looking at her from across a half mile of river.

Father grunted. "There's prizes and there's prizes," said he. "This one may cost us more'n she's worth."

"What d'ye mean, Father?" said I. "Are ye not glad the *Hannah*'s took?"

"Will, supposin' you were Sir Henry Clinton —"

"I hope I'd hang myself," I said.

"A very patriotic sentiment, I'm sure," said Father, sniffing in that way he had for showing his appreciation of foolishness. "But, seriously, if you were Clinton, and you'd been waitin' for the *Hannah* to turn up with her cargo, and ye learned that a Yankee privateer had seized her, what would you do?"

I scratched my head and thought for a bit. Then I said, "I guess if I were Clinton, I'd want to punish them that took my ship."

Father nodded. "So it strikes me. Those folks that are singin' Captain Saltonstall's praises today may sing to another tune shortly."

More wonderment. Should Saltonstall have let the *Hannah* go? I couldn't see any sense in that. Yet, Father had a point. Clinton could hardly be expected to swallow his loss with a smile.

"It's like crossin' a bull in a pasture, Will," Father said. "It ain't prudent, unless mebbe you can rely on a Jordan Freeman to run in and get you out of it. If Clinton decides to turn his troops loose on New London, we may rue the day that Dudley Saltonstall ever put to sea."

Well, it was beyond me. I had thought it was a good thing that Saltonstall had done. And here was Father turning my thoughts upside down and making me half believe it was a bad thing. I frowned and squirmed and wrestled with the notions warring in my head, then I brightened and said, "But if Clinton was to send troops, we'd train our guns on 'em and just blow 'em to atoms."

"If they would oblige us by holdin' still for it," replied Father. "Pray they don't come, boy, is all I can say. Just pray they don't come."

"May I go to see the *Hannah* anyway?"

Father grinned. "You don't let go easy, do ye, Will? Well, I suppose ye must go. But have a care ye don't get pushed into the river nor crushed in the throng. You're needed here, boy. You know that."

I didn't know it, but it was good to hear, especially from Father. I was pleased that he decided to let me go. It saved my having to disobey him, which I more than likely should have done under such a temptation, and it raised my stock around the house some, too. My sister Lucy was green with jealousy. She wanted to go, too, and for a time I was scared to death that I would be told off to take her with me. This was my adventure, by Moses, and I wasn't willing to have it spoilt by having to drag Lucy along.

"I think it is mean and cruel and unfair," Lucy declared, with some passion. "Just because ye're a boy doesn't mean ye're any better or any smarter or any more to be trusted. Besides, I'm older'n you, and if you can go, then I should be able to go, too."

Ordinarily, I would have dealt with such sass in the ordinary way. But I was on my dignity now, so I just said, "Ye'd better take it up with Father."

Her argument was all nonsense, of course. A boy is naturally smarter, better, and more to be trusted than a gal — or so I believed. But I commenced to sweat some for fear that Father might be persuaded of Lucy's outlandish notions. She brought it up for airing at supper, and Father, looking solemn as a judge, looked down the table at her and said, "Lucy, there's a deal of sense in what ye say."

I almost swallowed my spoon.

"But, ye see, Daughter, the only way a boy

can learn wisdom is if you put him in harm's way and see if he can get out of it without breaking his neck. A gal, now, is different. They are just naturally more civilized, and they ain't half the trouble to raise that a boy is."

Lucy smirked so it was enough to make me gag. "Then," said she, very hoity-toity, "why may I not go, Father?"

"Because it's my outin' and you ain't welcome," I sputtered.

"Not with your mouth full, boy," admonished my father. "You've sprayed bread puddin' over half the table. Besides, your sister was speakin' to me."

I clammed up, feeling pretty foolish, but anxious, too. That interruption just might have scuttled me.

But Father said, "The truth is, Lucy, ye're gettin' on for to be a young lady."

Ye gods! How could a body listen to such stuff and still eat?

"And," Father went on, "a lady don't go gallivantin' after curiosities. 'Tisn't proper. Is it, Mother?"

Mother, who was spooning mashed up carrots into Luke, looked up and said, "No, 'tisn't. 'Sides, I don't want a gal of mine to be standin' around on a dock to be leered at by common sailors and wharf rats."

"I guess Mr. Nathaniel Gallup wouldn't care much for that, either," declared my sister Eunice, with a knowing look at Lucy.

"You hush, you mean thing!" cried Lucy, going all red. "Make her hush, Ma."

"Hush, Eunice," said Mother, mildly, shoveling another load into Luke. "A lady doesn't tease, either."

"Well, then," said Father, pushing back from the table, "that settles it, I guess. I mean for my gals to grow up proper, like their mother. So there'll be no more teasin', and no gallivantin' either."

"Well, I guess I don't want to go anyway," said Lucy. "I just felt it was my sisterly duty to look after little Billy."

Little Billy! Je-rusalem! That was worth a worm down her back at least. Or maybe a snake in her clothes press. If I hadn't been so happy to escape taking her along, I might have kicked her under the table. But there was no sense in crowding my luck.

"You may go in the mornin', Will," said Father. "We'll contrive to spare ye from the Fort for one day, but we'll be obliged to stop your wages, you understand. No work, no pay. That's gospel. Or it ought to be."

"Thank'ee, Father," I said. "I'll work the harder the next day to make up for it."

Father rose and filled his pipe, getting ready

to take his usual evening walk down to the village. "And, Will, see ye take no short-cuts, hear?" He started out the door. "I don't want to hear ye was chased by a whale trying to go crosslots over Long Island Sound to save a penny on the ferry."

So soon as the door closed behind Father, Lucy put her fingers to her forehead like horns, and went, "Moo-oo-oo!"

Mother fetched her a whack, and I took some satisfaction from that. But I was still in the market for a worm, you can bet. Father may have hoped his gals would grow up to be ladies, but I would not have given two cents for his chances.

Next morning found me early up and out. I didn't mean to lose a minute of my opportunity, and I didn't care to listen to any more advice or warnings and such. If I ever have a boy, and I tell him he may do a thing, I mean to just lay back and let him do it. If he gets stomped by a bull or et by a whale, well, at least he will have had the fun of the thing up to that point, without it being spoiled by a lot of jawing.

The dew was still on the grass, and it seemed like only God and I were up. I liked that. I liked the feeling of having the first helping of the new day, and having more of it than anybody else.

I sauntered along down to the ferry, paid my cent, and was soon scudding across the Thames with only the sleepy-eyed ferryman for company. It was lovely to be out thus early, on the blue water under a blue sky. I remember wishing that the scow were a real ship, that we were bound away on a grand voyage, out to the open sea among the pirates and the porpoises and the perils of the deep. But we only cut across the river, and I hopped off below Winthrop's cove and walked on down the wharf to where the *Hannah* lay, a great oaken prisoner tied fast to the pilings.

A few New Londoners were abroad by now, and they had come down "to see the elephant," as the saying goes. One old codger was holding forth in his high cracked voice, telling how Saltonstall did it. Seeing as how Saltonstall wasn't there to correct him, he had it all his own way. But I was only half listening, so struck was I with the size of the vessel. She was a big one, and no mistake. I would have paid out what I had to see her under full sail, but even so it was a treat to look at her. I felt pretty small up alongside her, and when I gawked up at her rigging and thought of sailors climbing up to reef the sails in a blow, my stomach went queasy and I had to look away.

I prowled up and down the wharf, looking

her over from stem to stern, trying to picture myself in Saltonstall's place. Je-rusalem! What a prize! I'd count myself a clever sailor could I go out in a little privateer like the *Minerva* and come back with an ark like the *Hannah* in tow. I reckoned if Noah had had the *Hannah* he could have taken four of everything and still had room for Mrs. Noah and all their relations.

Pretty soon a squad of militia showed up, and their corporal set 'em to work unloading. Most of the goods had been carried off by this time, so there wasn't a need for many hands. I was sorry to have missed seeing the bulk of the plunder, but it was pleasant to lounge there in the warming sunlight and watch the men cart off bales and barrels and to try to guess what was in 'em.

More and more people came drifting down to the wharf, some on foot and some in carriages. There were ladies, too, but ye can bet I never told Lucy that. The men all looked and talked as knowledgeable as Solomon, but I guess Solomon wasn't the sailor Noah was, for I never heard so much nonsense in any one morning in my whole life. I judged that most of 'em wouldn't know a binnacle from a barnacle, but that didn't slow 'em down any. Maybe they fooled the ladies; they didn't fool me.

One elegant gentleman in a plum-colored coat was running on about Saltonstall's courage in the face of superior strength when an evil looking wharf rat nearby let out a whinny and said, "Superior strength! Why, it was like driving a pig to market. A fool can see the *Hannah* ain't a fightin' ship. Where's her guns? Ye don't call them toy cannon guns, do ye? A canoe would run circles around her. Give me a canoe and a brace of pistols, and I'll bring ye home such a tub as that is every time."

The elegant gentleman was pretty put out, and he muttered something about teaching somebody some manners. But he muttered it pretty softly. The lady with him said, "Ignore the fellow, Elnathan. Let us drive along home."

But that wasn't so easily done, for the wharf was so crowded by this time that there wasn't room to turn his horse. So the elegant gentleman just had to sit there and endure the sneers of the wharf rat. It wasn't comfortable for him, I promise ye.

I was beginning to feel the slightest bit uncomfortable myself, with all those people crowding around. I guessed I had seen what there was to see, and I began to think of getting along back to my own side of the river. Maybe it wasn't so much of an adventure as I had thought it would be, but I had done it, and that was the main thing. I was satisfied and ready to go home. But getting through that crowd was like swimming against the tide. I was obliged to put my head down and just wade in. It was slow work, and painful, too, for I was barefoot as usual, and I got trod on more than once. But I was making progress. Then I ran up against something pretty solid, and I heard a familiar voice say, "Ye can't go through me, Billy Latham, and ye can't go over me. Reckon ye'll just have to alter your course and go around."

"Jordan!"

" 'Mornin', Billy," said Jordan, grinning down on me. "Your pa know ye're here?"

"He does. The Colonel know you're here?"

Jordan nodded. "He sent me across on business this morning, so I thought I might as well take in the sights while I was about it."

I was glad to see Jordan, and I think he was glad to see me. His smile lighted his whole face, and the pressure of his huge hand on my shoulder was warm and firm.

"Guess you're about ready to go home," he said.

"I have seen what there is to see," I said. "If I can wriggle my way out of this — oh-oh. Jordan, look!"

Jordan's gaze traveled in the direction of

my pointing finger. "Colonel Harris!"

It was he, sure enough, dressed fit to kill and striding along at the head of a pack of his important friends, ordering folks to stand aside, give room, make way for him to pass.

"I do believe it is time to go," Jordan said, and he fairly dove into that throng, slicing out a path for me to follow. With a man as big as Jordan making my way for me, I had a pretty smooth passage and didn't get stepped on more than two or three times at most. We were soon clear and standing well apart from the spectators. I felt as though I could breathe again.

"D'ye reckon he saw us, Billy?" asked Jordan.

I said I didn't think so, that he was too busy being important to have time to notice us.

"Well, I'm glad I saw him. Reckon mebbe I won't be goin' back to Groton directly, after all."

"Why not, Jordan?"

"Well, boy, I just remembered some other business I got to tend to on this side o' the river." Jordan patted me on the arm. "You go 'long to the ferry and I'll see you sometime."

"I've got all day, Jordan. If ye want company —"

Jordan rubbed his chin. Then he rubbed

the back of his neck. Then he squinted up at the wispy mares' tails trailing across the bright sky. Then he looked at me and said, "I wasn't lookin' for no company, Billy."

"Oh." I felt pretty small. I guess I must have looked it, too, because a smile broke out on Jordan's face, and the warm light of understanding glowed in his eyes.

"I guess if I was lookin' for company, I couldn't find no better," he said. He seemed to be turning something over in his mind. At last, he whacked me on the back and said, "Come along, then, Billy. I reckon I could use some company after all."

"Where we goin', Jordan?" said I, feeling light and glad, and skipping along to keep pace with his stride.

"Goin' to Colonel Harris's place, Billy."

"Colonel — ! But — but, Jordan, he's back there. Colonel Harris is on the wharf. He won't be to home."

Jordan squeezed my neck in the crook of his arm and grinned down at me, his eyes fairly dancing with mischief. "That's the best and the only time to go callin' at the Colonel's place, Billy — when the Colonel ain't home."

CHAPTER VI

Well, I was some staggered, I can tell ye. What on earth was Jordan thinking of? He'd already got Colonel Harris down on him for refusing to fight Tom Wansuc. It seemed to me to be flying in the face of certain disaster to go poking around in the enemy's camp. Plain sense told me I'd do better to hop on the ferry and get along back to my side of the river. But I had more or less pushed Jordan into letting me tag along. There was no decent way of backing down now.

Jordan's long legs fairly ate up the road, and I was all but trotting to keep up with him. He didn't seem to share my worries any. If he was a coward for not fighting with Tom, I had to allow he was about the bravest coward going. He was actually humming as we hurried along.

Colonel Harris's fine house was situated on Town Hill, almost directly opposite Fort Nonsense. We had not a long walk but a steep one, and it was warmish. Still, I'd have been all of sweat had it been as cold as Christmas. If Jordan was a coward, he wasn't the only one. I reckoned Harris would skin us alive if he found us hanging about his place. And what would Father say then?

As we neared the house, Jordan seemed of a mind to be more prudent, for all his devil-may-care attitude. "Let's just slide on by," he said, "and go 'round by the barn."

I followed, trembling in all my bones.

"You lay low," Jordan said, and I ducked down and hugged the weathered boards. Jordan cupped his hands to his mouth and gave out low and clear with the call of the whip-poor-will.

It was a pretty good call. Of course, no whip-poor-will would be whistling at that time of day, as anybody with any sense would know. But it sounded sure enough like one all the same. Three times Jordan whistled, then he crouched down beside me and waited. In a minute, I heard a door bang shut, then there was the sound of footsteps on gravel. Nearer they came, and nearer. Then they stopped, and I heard a soft voice say, "Jordan?"

" 'Round here," Jordan said. And around the corner of the barn stepped one of the prettiest women I ever hope to see. She was about as dark as Jordan, tall and straight as a hemlock, and graceful as a willow. Her bared arms were slender and well turned, and she was shapely as a man could wish. She carried her head high, but there was in her eyes an expression of such sweetness and such warmth as would melt the heart of a banker. Even in the patched and faded calico she wore, she was a beauty such as even a boy so young as I could not help but admire.

" 'Mornin', Sally," said Jordan.

"Oh, Jordan." She flung her arms around him and hugged him tight. Then, over his shoulder, she noticed me looking on with considerable interest, and she let out a gasp of surprise.

"What's wrong?" said Jordan, as Sally stepped back from the circle of his arms.

She pointed to me and said, "Who is that?"

Jordan, laughing, turned to look at me. "Why, that's Billy Latham," he said. "He's the boy that got me my freedom. Billy, say hello to Sally."

I ducked my head and said, "How do?"

Sally smiled at me in a way that made my knees go weak. "So you are Billy Latham," said she. "I'm proud to meet you."

"Me too," I said. And they both laughed. But it wasn't the mean kind of laugh some grownups have when they think a boy has done or said something foolish. It was friendly, and kind of shared-like, so as to take me in.

Jordan slipped his arm around Sally's waist

and said, "Billy, I'd be more'n grateful if you was to take up sentry duty at the far corner of the barn and let out a yip if you see anybody comin'. Me and Sally has got to have a talk."

I nodded and went to take up my post, but I was indifferent sharp about it, and I expect a whole regiment of Hessians could have stole a march on me if they'd have wanted to. Jordan had said that he and Sally had some talking to do. I didn't hear much talk. But I did see more hugging and kissing and carrying-on than ever I had seen in all my days. I was scandalized, I can tell ye. It was almost enough to make me hide my eyes. I was pretty certain such goings-on weren't proper, but they were more than middling interesting. All this hugging and such was a new thing to me, and all I can say is that it was a good thing that no one did come along, because it is more than doubtful that I'd have seen 'em.

I have to admit I was surprised at Jordan, and a little disappointed. I didn't take much stock in gals myself, and it troubled me to see a great strapping fellow like Jordan lallygagging after a woman. I commenced to wonder if he hadn't maybe gone soft. It was hard enough to square the Jordan that saved me from Old Caesar with the Jordan that refused to wrestle Tom Wansuc, without having to reconcile this kind of foolishness.

Oh, Sally seemed nice enough. And she was more than pretty, I'd give her that. But she was a gal. And from my experience, a gal wasn't worth ten minutes of a fellow's time. Ye can't go fishing with a gal; you can't hunt with 'em, nor fight with 'em, nor anything that amounts to shucks. Or so I thought then.

I was beginning to get restless. It seemed to me we had been there a mortal long time, and my interest in the whole proceedings was dwindling fast. Then I heard a woman holler from the house:

"Sal-lee! You, Sal! Drat the gal! Where's she got to?"

I guessed it must be Mrs. Harris. Jordan hugged Sally some more, and there was a good bit of kissing, too, but it looked like we were finally going. Jordan beckoned to me, and I trotted over.

"We'll be movin' on now, Billy," he said.

"Good."

Sally smiled at me, and then she did a strange thing. She took my face in both her hands and said, "I'm glad I met you, Billy. I thank you for comin' along with Jordan, today."

"Sal-lee! Where are you?"

"I have to go," Sally said. "Good-bye, Jordan. Billy, you keep an eye on him, for me."

"Reckon he can take care of himself," said

I, more gruffly than I had intended.

Sally laughed. "Lord knows, he's big enough."

"Sal-lee!"

"Oh, land! Jordan, good-bye. Come see me when you can." And she kissed him and flew off down the path.

"Oh, there ye are, Sal. Where on earth have you been? I been callin' and callin' —"

Jordan nudged me in the short ribs and led the way back down to the waterfront, and I just trudged along beside him in silence.

Jordan had come over in a johnboat belonging to Colonel Ledyard, so I was a cent ahead on the trip back. At his bidding, I hopped in and got situated, then Jordan pushed us off the mud flat and leaped in and started pulling for the opposite shore. You get a fine view of Fort Griswold from the river, and it gave me a comfortable feeling to look up and see cannon arrayed along the rampart, and the flag floating lazy on the soft westerly breeze.

"What did ye think of her, Billy?" Jordan said, giving his oars a rest.

"Who?"

"Who? Sally, that's who. What did ye think of her?"

"She's awful pretty, Jordan."

"Ain't she, though?" Jordan smiled and shook his head. "Lord, it makes me feel good just to look at her. She liked you, too, boy. I could tell."

"Did she?"

"Oh, yes. I could see that straight off. Sally ain't a gal to hide her feelin's."

Well, I guessed I knew that, what with all that hugging and kissing going on right before my eyes. But I didn't think it polite to mention it, so I just grunted.

"Yessir," Jordan said, "she sure enough likes you. And that's a good sign."

"It is?"

"Surely. A man can tell a lot about a gal by the way she behaves to his friends. Can't be no happiness with a woman that don't like your friends, that's certain."

"I — I reckon not," said I, feeling none too comfortable with the course of this conversation.

Jordan laughed, and his laughter was good to hear. I couldn't help but join in.

"Oh, Billy, Billy," he said, shaking his head, "I tell ye the truth, I hope our baby turns out to be a boy like you."

"Baby? What — what baby you talkin' about, Jordan?"

"Why, our baby. Sally's and mine."

Whoa up, Billy, thinks I to myself. Go slow. This was all moving too fast for me. "Jordan, is — is Sally goin' to have a baby?"

" 'Pears likely."

"But — but you ain't — you ain't —"

"Ain't what, Billy?"

"Well, I mean, you ain't married, Jordan. Are ye?"

"Good as, I reckon."

Lord A'mighty! I was stunned for fair. I didn't know much, but I knew that this was plain sinful. Why, Jordan would more than likely go to Hell! Indeed, I couldn't see how he could avoid it. Yet, there he sat, just as cheerful and easy as if there wasn't a thing on his conscience or worry on his mind. I judged he must be what the Reverend Mr. Kinne called a hardened sinner. There wasn't the least sign in him of anything like shame. And Sally! Why, to look at her, ye wouldn't think her less than a black angel in calico. Yet she was damned, too, and she didn't seem to care anymore than Jordan did.

A great trembling seized me, and I felt cold and sick and afraid. Mr. Kinne had preached a considerable good deal about Hell, and I felt I had more than a passing acquaintance with conditions there. The thought of Jordan, my friend, roasting and sizzling forever and ever, without any hope of an end to torment, fairly curdled my blood.

And what of me? By rights, I shouldn't be associating with hardened sinners. If Mr.

Kinne knew, if Father knew — but then, God already knew. He knew. And He, no doubt, was weighing me in the balance, watching to see which way I'd jump. I would either have to cut Jordan's acquaintance, or risk going to Hell along with him. And Sally. Oh, Lord, what was I to do?

Jordan, all unmindful of the turmoil going on inside me, took up his oars once more, rattling on just as if there wasn't the slightest thing amiss. "When I first met Sally," he said, "I knew I was a gone goose. I'd come over with Colonel Ledyard on a matter of business with Colonel Harris, and there was Sally, lookin' just as pretty as she did today, out back a-feedin' the chickens."

" 'What are you lookin' at?' she says to me, as pert as ye please.

"And I said, 'I'm lookin' at the prettiest gal I ever did see.' And from then on, it was just as natural as rollin' downhill. I'd light out every blessed chance I got, and just help myself to the loan of this good ol' johnboat, and scoot across the river to see my gal. Reckon I've rowed above a thousand miles just goin' back and forth to visit Sally."

"Well, but, Jordan," said I, finding my voice at last, "why didn't you and Sally just get married?"

"Married? How was we to do that, I'd like

to know. She's the property of old Colonel Harris. And I was the property of Colonel Ledyard. I was. But I ain't no more." He grinned at me, and winked. "Nossir, I ain't no more. I'm a free man and workin' for wages. Every week I lay a little bit by, and bimeby I'm goin' to have enough to buy my Sally free. Then we can talk about marryin'."

"Lordy, Jordan. Suppose Colonel Harris won't sell her to ye? He mightn't, ye know. Especially after ye — disappointed him up to the Fort."

Jordan tapped his forehead and gave me a wise old look. "I know what you're a-sayin', Billy. But Jordan ain't a total fool, if I can't read nor write. What I'll do is, I'll get the money together, and then I'll ax someone else to buy Sally for me. I expect the Colonel would do it for me, if I axed him. He's fond of me, is Colonel Ledyard. And I guess he don't think much more o' that Colonel Harris than I do. Yessir, I expect he'd do it. I know he would.

"But first I got to get up the money." Jordan's smile faded, and he looked pretty solemn. "Got to do it quick, too. I want my child born free, Billy. And I don't want to lose him or Sally. She's bound to start showin' her condition afore long, and that old devil Harris, he's just mean enough to sell her hisself if he takes a notion to. A strong handsome gal like Sally would fetch more'n a hundred dollars, I guess. 'Course, she wouldn't bring down so much with a baby to care for; but if she was to be sold off afore anyone could tell she was goin' to have the baby, old Harris could just pocket the money, and if the new owner hollered he'd been stung, why, old Harris could tell him to go to Jericho."

"Do you have a hundred dollars, Jordan?"

"Who, me?" Jordan looked at me as if I'd gone crazy. "Where'd I get a hundred dollars? I got the purse your pa gave me, and the little I've laid by my wages. Altogether, I got mebbe twelve dollars."

Twelve dollars was a lot of money to me, but it was a long way from a hundred, a mortal long way. "Lord, Jordan," I said, "how are you goin' to raise the rest of it?"

"Just keep on workin', I guess. It's the onliest thing I know."

"Couldn't ye mebbe borry the money?"

"Who'd lend money to me?"

"I would, if I had any."

Jordan grinned.

"I will have some, too," I said. "Nothing like a hundred dollars, mebbe, but I will have somethin'. Father's payin' me for my work at the Fort. When I get my money, you're welcome to it, Jordan."

"Thank'ee, Billy. It's good to know I can

look to you if I need to."

"Jordan?"

"Hm?"

"Jordan, if ye need money so bad, how come — how come ye backed away from wrestling Tom Wansuc?"

Jordan stopped rowing. His mouth went all grim and severe, and his eyes bored into me like augurs. Then he heaved a great sigh, rested on his oars and said, "Billy, if I ever want anything that bad, I hope I may die."

"But a gold piece, Jordan. That would —"

"Boy, don't you think I would like to have that gold piece? And don't you think I need it?" Jordan sounded really angry, and I felt sorry and scared, and I wished I hadn't brought it up.

I must have looked it, too, for Jordan's face softened some, and he even smiled a little. "Billy," he said, "there's some things a man don't do. Not if he's a man. One thing is, he don't shame his friend. And another is, he don't shame himself. If I was to take old Harris's damned money, what would that say about the kind of friend I am to Tom? And what would it say about Jordan Freeman?

"A gold piece can't buy me a friend like Tom Wansuc. But that partic'lar gold piece could have cost me my friend, if I'd been fool enough to take it. And it could have cost me my freedom, too."

"How is that, Jordan? Colonel Ledyard gave you your papers."

"Bein' free ain't only a matter of papers, boy. Nossir. It's bein' able to stand up and say no to a man that would try to buy a performance from you, as if you was a trained bear or a racehorse. If I'd have gone and wrassled Tom to amuse the colonel's toney friends, I'd have been more of a slave than ever I was when I belonged to Colonel Ledyard. If I'd a-done that, I don't think I could ever hold my head up again. You can see that, can't ye?"

I nodded.

"Good." Jordan smiled. "If ye couldn't, I'd be dreadful disappointed. It matters to me that my friends can see the right of things. It surely does."

He rowed on, not saying anything. And there wasn't anything I could say. My head was all in a muddle. Here was Jordan, bound for Hell just as sure as sunrise, saying it mattered that I see the right of things. No matter which angle I approached it from, I just couldn't fathom it. But I couldn't let it rest, either. I admired Jordan. I couldn't help liking him. I surely didn't want for him to go to Hell, and I didn't want to drop his acquaintance, that was certain. But then, I didn't want to go to Hell, either.

I was in over my depth. I decided that the only thing for me to do was to sound out Father. If anybody could shed light on all this, he could. I hoped God wouldn't object if I was to reserve my judgement till then.

"Well, here we are, dry and whole and back the same day," said Jordan, as our boat nosed in to the bank.

We got out and started walking up the hill. "I'm glad I run into you today, Billy," Jordan said, laying his big hand on my shoulder. "It purely pleased me to have ye meet my Sally."

"Thank'ee, Jordan. I'm glad I got to meet her."

We walked along easy, the sun at our backs, enjoying the cool of the late afternoon breeze blowing in off the Sound. Then I said, "Jordan?"

"Yes, Billy?"

"You weren't really afraid to wrestle Tom, then, were ye?"

Jordan squeezed my neck in the crook of his arm and said, "Onliest thing I was afraid of was the temptation. I surely could have used that gold piece."

"Jordan?"

"Hm?"

"D'ye think ye could whip him?"

"Who?"

"Tom Wansuc."

Jordan threw back his head and laughed. "Billy, Billy," he said, "that's somethin' you and I ain't never goin' to know."

CHAPTER VII

I rather shone at supper that night. Mother and the gals were curious to hear all about the *Hannah*, and I polished up a pretty good account of her. Not that I lied, mind, but I did lay it on pretty thick about the size of the vessel and the quantity of plunder she yielded. I didn't let on about meeting Sally, but I did tell about meeting Jordan and coming back with him. It was pleasant having an audience, and I just gabbled away like an auctioneer.

Father didn't seem to take a share in the general interest, though. He stayed pretty quiet through the meal. I knew how he felt about the taking of the *Hannah*, of course, though I couldn't wholly understand it. He said he was glad I had my outing and got home in one piece, but he seemed more occupied with his own thoughts than with anything I had to tell.

When we'd polished off the rhubarb pie Mother had baked for us, Father rose and announced he was off for his accustomed walk.

"May I come with you, Father?" said I.

"Ain't you tired from your day's ramble, Will?"

"Not really, Father. And, well, there's something I want to talk over with you."

He nodded. "Come along, then. Don't want to miss the sunset."

I don't know shucks about painting pictures, and I can't draw worth a hill of beans. But if I could, if I were an artist, I know I would just have to try to capture the colors of a summer sky at sundown. I'd make the Thames my foreground, and maybe show the houses and shops along the New London shore, with a ship or two thrown in for good measure. Then I would just haul off and let fly with every blessed color I had to show that sky. There is no point in tossing off words like "beautiful" or "lovely" or "grand." They don't come close. You have to see the pinks and reds, the violets and the dozen different shades of blue, the orange and the gold, all running together, yet somehow separate and distinct from one another. It can't be written, and I doubt it can be painted either. But if I could paint, I'd have to try.

Father and I strolled along under such a sky, down to where the water laps the great slanting slabs of stone that slope down to the river's edge. We sat ourselves down on a convenient ledge and just drank in all that beauty, not saying anything, only watching in silent wonder as the sun slid down the flaming sky to dip in the shining sea.

Father drew on his reeky old clay pipe and let out a great cloud of smoke, sighed contentedly, and said, "Well, Will, what's on your mind?"

"Salvation," I said.

Father grunted. "Big subject," he said. "I wonder you don't take it up with Mr. Kinne."

"I did think of that," I said, "but, well, I guess I can talk easier with you."

"Why, Will, that's a handsome thing for you to say, whether ye know it or not." He placed a hand on my knee. "Ye know, bein' a father is one of those things a man has to learn as he goes along. There ain't any apprenticeships for fathers, and there's no colleges that I know of where they can teach you how to go about it. Lord knows, there's been times when I've wished there was.

"But I guess if you feel ye can talk to your father about a thing like salvation I must be doin' a passable job. Pure luck, more'n likely. But I'm glad all the same."

I didn't know what to say to that. Father was — well, Father. I never thought of him in any other light. I never wondered whether he was a good father or a poor one. He was just — my father. And I liked him a lot, and admired him, and never questioned his style of fathering. It came as a surprise to me to hear that he even thought about it. Back then, I suppose, I just assumed that all fathers were like mine. I know better now, and I wish there was some way of telling him so without making both of us feel foolish.

"Well, fire away, Will," he said, taking a pull on his pipe. "Only don't expect too much by way of answers. I ain't a preacher nor a scholar, only a pretty ordinary sort of man."

"Well, Father, if a friend of yours was behavin' contrary to the Commandments —"

"Most of 'em are, one way and another," Father put in, chuckling. "But excuse me, Will. Go on."

"Well, I mean, supposin' you knew that a friend of yours was livin' sinful and was plainly bound for Hell. Would you feel obliged to cut his acquaintance?"

Father took his time replying. He scratched his head and rubbed his chin and sniffed two or three times in that Yankee way of his. Then he said, "Will, I think I know you pretty well. And I'm pretty certain you wouldn't ask a question like that without there was a real reason. So I guess that some friend of yours is gone off the straight-and-narrer. That the way of it?"

I nodded.

"Hum. Well." Father puffed hard on his pipe, putting up a cloud that all but hid his face. "I don't want to know who it is, and I don't want to know what he's doing. But tell me this, Will. He hasn't tried to persuade you to do anythin' ye shouldn't, has he?"

"No, Sir."

"That's good. Because a friend that would do that is no friend a-tall." Father stared off at the western horizon for a long moment, then he said, "Friendship's a great gift, Will. It ain't somethin' to be let go of lightly. Some would say it ain't proper to be friends with an out-and-out sinner, but who ain't a sinner, hey? I seem to recall that 'In Adam's fall, we sinned all.' Or so it said in my primer when I was at school. And if we was to rule out sinners as friends, we'd be dreadful lonesome, Will. Dreadful lonesome."

"Guess so," I said, slapping at a mosquito as it whined past my ear.

"Seems to me, too, that I've heard Mr. Kinne read out of the Book how the bigwigs of His time was always jawin' at Jesus for keepin' company with sinners. You've heard that, haven't ye?"

I allowed I had.

"Well, then. I guess it don't take a scholar to see the right of it. Jesus talked some pretty brisk language to those folks that were so all-fired righteous about the kind o' company He kept. He called 'em vipers and hypocrites and one or two other things that wasn't so pleasant. And He went right on bein' friends with some pretty lowdown people."

"I remember," said I, feeling brighter. "There was tax-collectors and harlots and —"

"Yes, yes," said Father. "He was friend to all kinds. And if we are to call ourselves Christians, why, I guess that means we have to try to behave like Him. It don't mean we have to get down in the mud and waller with the man that's actin' like a hog, but it means we don't judge him and we don't condemn him, and we don't leave him out in the cold, neither.

"Drat these m'skeeters!" Father waved his hand in the air and blew out a monstrous cloud of smoke to drive the pests away. "Let's start for home, Will, afore they eat us alive."

As we strolled through the deepening twilight, I felt the weight of Father's hand on my shoulder. It was a good feeling, and I took comfort from it as much as from his words.

"I dunno that I have solved anything for ye, Will," he said. "I'm not sure but what this is a thing ye'd have to solve for yourself anyway. But I will say that there ain't a time when a friend matters more than when a body's in trouble. And there ain't any trouble to compare with bein' at odds with the Almighty."

"Thank'ee, Father," said I, peering up at him in the twilight. "I'm glad I talked this out with ye."

"So'm I, boy," Father said. "If it helped any, I'm more'n glad."

"Oh, it helped, Father. It helped a good deal. I know now that I have to stand by my friend."

"You do that, Will. And pray that when the time comes when you need a friend, as it surely will, there'll be a fellow the likes o' Billy Latham to stand by you."

"Father?"

"Yes, Will?"

"Couldn't you give Lambo his freedom?"

"Lambo?" Father halted and stared down at me. "But I thought — Hem! I mean, whatever put ye in mind of Lambo, Will?"

"Oh, I — I guess I been thinkin' about him ever since Colonel Ledyard set Jordan free. The Colonel said it seemed strange to him that he should be ready to fight and die for freedom and yet keep a man in bondage."

"He said that, did he?"

"Yes, Sir. And, well, you have done some fightin' for the same thing, and it struck me —"

"Will, how old are you now?"

"Be twelve next month, Father. But —"

"Only twelve. Je-rusalem, boy! I expect you'll end up a member o' Congress, or at least a lawyer."

"I mean to be a soldier, Father. Like you. But Lambo —"

"Has Lambo said anything about this to you?"

"No, Sir."

"This is your own notion, then."

"Yes, Sir."

"Humph." Father commenced walking again, but slowly, his hands clasped behind his back, his eyes fixed on the road before him. "Well, Will, I don't know but what the Colonel's right. We've told King George and the whole wide world that we b'lieve all men are created equal. We didn't say all white men, or even all Americans, we said all men. And if we didn't mean it, then we shouldn't have said it."

"Then ye'll free Lambo, Father?"

"Hum, well, I'd certainly be inclined to. Indeed, I guess I'd have to, or else swear off these United States and go over to the other side like Benedict Arnold. But, the thing is, Lambo belongs to your grandpa, Will. He ain't mine to free."

"Oh."

"And your grandpa's awful set in his ways."

That was true enough. My grandfather, Deacon Jonathan Latham, was a stern old gentleman, long on virtue but short of temper. As a small boy, I thought him a regular fire-eater. And as I got older, I did not change my opinion significantly. I didn't fear him, exactly, but I made it my business to steer wide of him whenever he came to call. Not that he was mean, or ever unkind to me, ye understand, but he was just so forbidding and grim that I could not be in the same room with him without feeling like I had died and come to Judgement. And if Grandpa was doing the judging, well, a sinner like me wouldn't have a prayer.

"Tell ye what, Will," said my father, as we neared the house, "I will sound out your grandpa on this matter first chance I get. Don't say a word of it to Lambo, mind. No point in gettin' him stirred up. Just leave it to me, and I'll see if I can't find a way.

"Thing is, I have to go 'round-about with Grandpa. Worst thing ye can do with him is to tackle a thing head-on. It's his nature to dig in and resist. He can't help it." Father chuckled. "He's a tough old bird, my father. Got more backbone than most men half his age. And stubborn? I mean to say!

"Well, the worst that can happen is that we may have to wait till the old gentleman is called to his reward. Lambo'll be my property then, and I can free him in a minute. Meantime, he's well cared for, and he's eatin' reg'lar. There's many who'd like to be able to say as much, I guess."

"But ye will try to get him free?"

"I said so. And I will, one way or another. You must — Say, ain't that your friend Jordan comin' this way?"

It was Jordan, sure enough, and it was plain he'd come on purpose to see us, for he paused before our door and seemed about to go into the yard when he caught sight of Father and me and came over to us.

" 'Evenin', Jordan," said Father.

" 'Evenin', Cap'n Latham. 'Evenin', Billy."

"What brings ye here?" asked Father.

"The Colonel sent me, Cap'n. He axed me to ax you if Missus Latham could come up to the house."

"Is it Miss Sarah, Jordan?"

"Yessir. She's gone to glory, Cap'n. Poor little lady. Missus Ledyard is grievin' so bad, it breaks my heart to see her so. The Colonel thought your missus would —"

"Of course," said Father, "of course she'll come. You tell the Colonel I'll bring her along directly."

"Yessir, Cap'n. Thank'ee." Jordan heaved a great sigh. "Reckon I'd best get on back and see if I can't make myself useful."

"You do that," Father said. "And tell your — tell the Colonel I'm most dreadfully sorry."

Jordan nodded and walked off into the darkness.

Father shook his head. "This is hard news, boy," he said. "Poor Anna Ledyard. She set great store by Sarah. This'll surely break her heart."

"Mother will comfort her, Father," I said.

He nodded. "Ay-uh. Seems like folks always send for your mother when trouble comes, Will. I never see the beat of her for lendin' a helpin' hand or a kind word. If I ever did anything clever in my life, it was to marry your mother.

"Well, get along in, boy. You've had a long day and a full one. You need your sleep."

I was tired, but I couldn't get to sleep somehow. The moon was so bright, and my mind was taken up with so many things. Most of all, though, I thought of Sarah Ledyard.

I sat by my garret window, looking out on the moonlit night, feeling small and lonesome and strange. Sarah was dead. I hadn't known her all that well, but in a village so small as ours, you had to know just about everybody to some extent. She had been a pretty gal, and gay and sweet-tempered and good as gold. And she was dead.

She knew more now than the wisest man alive, more than Mr. Kinne or Governor Trumbull or any of 'em. She knew all that there is to know, and the only thing worth knowing.

The breeze from off the river billowed my curtain like the sail of a ship. I rested my chin on the sill, just gazing off into the mysterious dark, thinking the most melancholy kind of thoughts. It struck me that life was nothing but dying. As soon as child's born, it starts on its way to the grave. Maybe it'll live only ten years, or maybe a hundred, but ever since Adam, why, the whole human family has just been passing through this world, and none of 'em has ever stayed on.

Some day Father would die, and Mother, and Jordan, and everybody that was alive in the village that night. I would die, too. Some day. That gave me the goose bumps just to think it. I couldn't imagine the town without me in it. I couldn't imagine school in session, farmers plowing and reaping, ships going down the river, boys and girls at play, people moving in and out of the houses and the shops, and me not there to see it. And yet, barring the end of the world and the coming of Judgment, it was certain as sunrise that a time would come when I'd be lying out there at Packer's Rock, and the whole world would be ticking right along just as if I had never lived. I tell ye, it made me feel so solemn and so sad that real tears trickled down my face.

If I'd been a better sort of boy, I reckon I'd have wept for Miss Sarah, or for her mother. But I didn't. I wept for me.

Then, from somewhere close by, an owl whooed, and I felt prickles all over my scalp. I never could hear an owl without thinking of ghosts. Lordy, thought I, can that be Sarah?

Then I told myself not to talk stuff. A good gal like Sarah, why, she was already outfitted with wings and a harp, and was no doubt rejoicing in the Kingdom that very minute.

Folks who become haunts, I knew, were those that misbehaved themselves so in this life that they couldn't rest easy in the ground, but went about nights whooing and scaring the daylights out of people.

I got to thinking about that, and I began to wonder if maybe that was what lay in store for me and for Jordan. We were a pair of reprobates, and no mistake. Chances were better than fair that he and I would wind up as haunts and go flitting around and caterwauling and making folks jump clean out of their skins.

That kind of cheered me. There were two or three folks I could think of straight off that I'd take a deal of pleasure in haunting. And I was sure Jordan had some bills of his own to pay. Why, he and I could fly over to New London and sit on Colonel Harris's rooftop and whoo down his chimney till the old walrus howled for mercy. But we'd never let up on him till he changed his ways, and got religion. That'd be a fine joke on him, I guessed.

I felt so much better, just thinking about that, that I got up and hopped into bed and slept clear through to morning.

CHAPTER VIII

I felt awkward when Colonel Ledyard turned up at the Fort the first time after Miss Sarah's burial. Father went over and shook his hand and said, "Well, Neighbor, the Lord giveth and the Lord taketh away."

"Amen, Neighbor," said Ledyard, his manner composed and even cheerful, though his face was pale and there were dark rings under his eyes. "I'm obliged to you and Eunice for your kindness, Will."

"Sorry we couldn't do more," Father said. "How's Anna?"

Ledyard nodded. "Bearing up, Sir. She has another life to think about these days." Then he noticed me and said, "Good morning, Will."

"I — I'm awful sorry, Colonel," I said, scarce able to look him in the face.

Sick and sad as he was, and worried about a thousand things, Ledyard bent down and, with the kindest smile imaginable, he said, "I know ye are, Will. I know ye are. And Mrs. Ledyard and I are thankful to ye for comin' to the church and all. It was a manly thing for you to do."

Well, I hadn't wanted to, I can tell ye. I didn't know how to deal with it, and I was miserable the whole time, what with seeing the coffin and knowing who was inside it, and seeing poor Mrs. Ledyard and hearing her sobs, and listening to Mr. Kinne for above an hour in that sweltering meeting house talking about how we had all better repent while there was yet time because Death comes like a thief in the night. I felt so bad I even pitied that sauce-box Miss Deborah, for all she was so different from Miss Sarah and so mean. I only went because Father said I must. It wasn't anything to brag on. But now that the Colonel had said he was glad I'd gone, I felt some better.

"Well, Captain Latham," the Colonel said, "there's work to be done. The war's not over yet."

We were all kept middling busy through the rest of July. There had been rumors of the wildest kind all that summer, and the taking of the *Hannah* seemed to stir up more. There was talk of raids, talk of invasion, talk of Clinton and Arnold, of Hessians and Reg'lars, of victory and defeat. After a time, we got so we didn't credit any of it.

But the war was never far away. It colored every hour of every day in that summer of

’81. We had lived with it so long that even the oldest inhabitant found it hard to recall a time of peace. And for one so young as I was, why, I couldn’t imagine living in another kind of time. I just knew that I would grow up to fight lobsterbacks. What else was there for a Yankee boy to do? And I looked forward to it. I believed then that everybody else did, too.

One afternoon, in prime green-apple time, Jordan turned up at the Fort with a cartload of lumber needed to repair the barracks. His errand done, he caught up with me at the well and said, “Billy, what’s your views on fishin’?”

“Guess I’d sooner fish than eat,” I said.

Jordan grinned. “I knew it!” he cried. “I told myself that Billy Latham is just the sort o’ boy who would like fishin’. I bet you’re a good fisherman, too.”

“Reckon so,” I said.

“There now,” said Jordan. “Don’t tell me Jordan Freeman don’t know a fisherman when he sees one.”

Well, I couldn’t argue with him, so I just squinted up at him and said, “What’s on your mind, Jordan?”

“Fish,” he said. “And fishin’. Are you of a mind to go?”

“When?”

"Tonight. Tom and me, we got us the loan of a rowboat, and we mean to catch ourselves a mess of pout and eels and whatever else is bitin' over to Poquonnock Pond. We'd be glad of your company, if ye'd care to come along."

If I cared to! "Let me ask Father," I said.

"He's over yonder with Sergeant Avery, next the powderhouse."

"I ain't meanin' to ask him now," I said. "I mean to wait till he's had his supper and is feelin' full and contented."

Jordan chuckled. "Makes sense," he said. "I'll swing past your house this evenin' and whistle for ye."

"Good. I'll come if I can."

Jordan turned to go, then he stopped, turned back and said, "Somebody axed to be remembered to ye."

"Who was that?"

"Sally."

"Oh. How-how is she, Jordan?"

"Pretty smart, I guess. She's took quite a fancy to you, Billy."

"I like her, too," I said.

"I'm glad."

"Jordan?"

"Yes, Billy?"

"Have ye been able to lay up any more money?"

He shook his head, the smile fading from

his face. "Nothin' to speak of. It comes awful slow."

"What are ye goin' to do — if ye can't raise it in time?"

Jordan shrugged. "I don't rightly know, Billy. If it comes to it, I may just have to run off with her."

My stomach turned a somersault and tied itself up in a knot. "Run off?"

"If I have to."

"But — but, Jordan, they'd come lookin' for you. And when they caught you, they'd put you in jail."

"I expect they would, if they caught us, Billy. That Colonel Harris ain't a man as would take kindly to losin' his belongin's. Reckon we'd have to run fast and far to give that old fox the slip.

"Well, no sense in frettin' about that today. Time enough when we come up against it." Jordan smiled. "Don't you go worryin' your head about it, Billy. Let's go fishin' tonight; you can worry tomorrow, if you've a mind to."

He left then, and I went back to lugging my buckets — and to worrying. I couldn't help it. It was plain to me that a storm was brewing, and I was dead certain that Jordan and Sally were headed for big trouble. What wasn't plain, no matter how I kept churning it over and over in my head, was how I could help, what I could do to keep that storm from breaking.

Directly after supper that night, I tested the air and judged it about right for seeking favors.

"My," I said, rubbing my belly, "that sure was a fine supper."

"You et enough," said Lucy, crinkling up her nose at me.

"Never you mind," Mother said. "Billy's a growing boy, and he's been working hard all summer. It's right that he should eat hearty."

I was of a mind to say something sharp to Lucy, but sense told me it was the wrong road. So I just ignored her and, smiling up at Mother, I said, "Yes, Ma'am, there's nobody in the whole village can cook as good as you."

Mother sniffed. "It's a mighty small village," she said. But I could see she was pleased.

"Yessir, there's nothin' goes down so good as a plate of your fried chicken, unless mebbe it's a plate of your fried fish."

Mother smiled. "I'm afraid we won't see much fish in this house this summer. The flounder are about gone as it is, and anyway, there is precious little fishin' done nowadays for fear of the British fleet."

I nodded, striving to look knowing. Then

I said, "There's still panfish, though. Mebbe it ain't as fine as the saltwater kind, but a mess of perch or hornpout fried up in batter makes a middlin' good supper anytime."

"That does sound good," Father put in. Something in his tone made me glance over at him, and I could see he was trying to hide a grin about half as wide as a barn door. He caught me looking, and he kind of pursed his mouth and took to studying the beams in the ceiling.

"Well," said Mother, a mite tartly, "it may sound good, but a body can't cook what a body doesn't have. And I'm not about to go fishin', I can promise ye that. Nasty worms!"

"Why, Mother, if ye've a mind to have some fish," said I, sweet and innocent as you please, "I would be willin' to try my luck."

"I'd say ye been tryin' it right along," muttered Father, just loud enough for me to hear. I felt my ears burn, but I pretended not to notice.

"What's that ye say, Will?" asked my Mother.

"Oh, nothin'," Father said. "Just thinkin' out loud, I guess."

"Humph." Mother eyed him suspiciously for a bit, then she turned her attention back to me. "You ain't by any chance tryin' to get leave to go fishin', are ye, Billy?"

"Why, no, Ma'am," said I, as though that were the farthest thing from my mind. "It's just that when ye talked about how good a mess of fish would taste, I thought —"

"Seems to me it wasn't I who talked of cravin' fish," she said, folding her arms across her middle and looking right through me. "Seems to me it was somebody else said that."

"Oh. Well, mebbe I misunderstood. I thought ye liked fish."

"Of course I like it, but —"

"Well, then, I'd be glad to try and catch ye some."

Mother sniffed. "Kind of you, I'm sure. But how can you get off to go fishin' when you're needed over to the Fort?"

"Oh, that's daytimes," I said. "No reason I couldn't go fishin' of an evening, is there?"

"Ye weren't thinkin' of any one evenin' in partic'lar, were ye, Billy?"

"Oh," said I, cool as anything, "one evenin's as good's another, so long as there ain't a thunderstorm. Fish don't bite worth shucks after a thunderstorm."

"Oh," said Mother. "I don't know why it struck me so, but I had the feelin' mebbe you were of a mind to go this evenin'."

I looked out the window, as though I was just now taking stock of the weather. "It does look like a prime evenin' for it," I said.

"Guess I could take any number of fish on a night like this."

"And I bet, if ever I was inclined to do so wicked a thing as bettin', that it would be a prime evenin' for fallin' into the pond and gettin' yourself drowned."

Lucy snickered, but Mother reached out and gave her hair a yank and said, "You hush."

"I'm a strong swimmer, Mother. You know that." I ached to give Lucy a kick, but there was too much at stake to risk it.

"What d'ye think, Will?" Mother asked Father.

"I think it's a prime evenin' for fishin'," he said.

"You would." Mother looked at my innocent upturned face, then back to Father. "You goin' with him?"

"Can't," he said. "I got business with Major Gallup this evenin'. Besides, I wasn't asked."

"Well, he can't go alone. There's got to be somebody there to fetch his corpse out of the water and cart it home."

My mother could be pretty humorous sometimes, for a mother.

"Oh," I said, careless-like, "I thought mebbe Jordan or Tom Wansuc would go along with me."

"Them heathens! My land, Billy, I don't know whether ye'll drown or hang. Imagine!

Traipsin' around with those two vagabones!"

"Now, Mother," Father said, "y'know very well that Jordan's a trusty fellow. So's Tom Wansuc, for that matter. And Billy wouldn't be here tonight, all full of chicken and corn chowder, if it hadn't a-been for Jordan."

"Seems to me he could find boys his own age to run with."

"Most of the village boys are all gone off to work on the farms," Father said. "Besides, Billy'll come to no harm travelin' with a friend like Jordan or Tom."

"Well-ll, I dunno." Mother shook her head. "I s'pose they're strong enough to lug the body home, anyway. But if he drowns himself, I'll never forgive ye for lettin' him go."

Father snorted. "Je-rusalem, Woman! Boys have been goin' fishin' for about a million years, I guess. There's lots worse mischief they could get into."

"As you should know, Will Latham. Well, if Jordan and that savage are goin', ye may as well go, Billy. I s'pose ye'd give me no peace till I gave in anyway. But — Hark! What's that?"

There was a rumble of wheels in the roadway, and a whip-poor-will called right outside our door. It must have been a powerful big whip-poor-will, for the sound carried clear back to the kitchen. Before I could make a move to cover my tracks, Mother was off to the window to peer out.

"Land o' Goshen!" she cried. "Billy Latham!"

"Yes, Ma'am?" I couldn't look at Father, nor could he look at me.

Mother marched back to the table and stood looking down at me most severely. "Think ye're clever, don't ye?"

"Ma'am?"

"Don't give me that saucer-eyed look, young man. Ye had this all arranged beforehand, you and your talk about my cookin'!"

"But ye do cook good, Mother. Don't she, Father?"

"Better'n anybody in the whole village," said he, cackling fit to bust. "Of course, it's a mighty small village."

Mother glared at him, but I could see her lips twitching, and I knew she'd be laughing in another minute. "I may be a fair hand to cook up a meal," said she, "but when it comes to cookin' up mischief, I don't expect to live to see the beat of my own boy."

"He is a middlin' shrewd plotter," Father said. And he and Mother both burst out laughing.

"Reckon I'd better get my pole," I said. "I don't want to keep the fish waitin'."

I skinned on out of the house while they were both enjoying themselves. It seemed like the right time to go.

"Hey, Billy," Jordan cried, as I nipped around from the back of the house with my fishing pole in my hand. "Hop up, and we'll go catch us a whale."

"Stir up the hoss, Jordan," said I, as I scrambled up onto the seat beside him. "Let's scratch dirt afore some folks change their minds."

"I hear ye, boy," said Jordan. "Gee-up, there, Dolly!"

We moved out pretty lively and, like Lot in the Bible, I didn't look back.

"What d'ye think of our boat, Billy?" Jordan asked, when we'd put a little distance between ourselves and the house.

I looked back at the wagon bed and saw a pretty little rowboat, painted white with dark green trim. "She's handsome," I said. "The Colonel's?"

"Yessir. He let me have the loan of it so's we can get out to where the big ones are. We'll have good fishin' tonight, I reckon."

Jordan guided the horse to the edge of the village, where Tom Wansuc lived in a little brown-shingled house, hardly any bigger than Jordan's cabin, but neat and civilized, with a fair-sized yard in front and a big garden out back. Tom was waiting in the doorway, and he lost no time in swinging up beside me on the seat. "How do, Billy," he said. "Jordan. Good night for to catch fish."

"You know it," Jordan said, smacking his lips. "I can just taste them fellers now, all hot and sizzlin' right from the pan. Mm-mmph! I mean to eat myself sick. And when I've done that, why, I'll just turn around and eat myself well again. Ha-ha!"

Even Tom laughed at that, if you can call it laughing. It was more like a series of grunts, and his face didn't change any, but for his eyes going brighter. As for me, I felt so free and silly and glad to be going that I reckon I'd have laughed at anything.

We rumbled along the road through Dark Hollow Woods, and in less than an hour, we raised the shore of the pond. Tom and Jordan lifted the boat down from the wagon and set her in the shallows, then I hopped in, then Jordan. Tom shoved us off, and sprang in light as a cat. Jordan took the oars and paddled us out to the middle of the calm, dark water.

It was getting dim. The sun had already dipped down under the hills, and the shadows were creeping through the woods to the eastern edge of the pond. The air was hushed, the water smooth as glass. But for the hum of night-flying insects and the sleepy chirp of the birds as they settled down for the night, there wasn't a sound to be heard. You felt you ought to whisper, if you ought to talk at all.

But Jordan was bent on business. He got his line baited and over the side in short order. "Oh, Mister Hornpout," he crooned, "here comes your dinner now."

Tom Wansuc and I got our lines in, and it was most pleasant just floating there on the pond, keeping one eye on the bobber and the other out for stars. I soon found myself floating in my thoughts, just drifting, drifting . . .

"First bite!" cried Jordan, startling me so I nearly jumped out the boat. He hoisted his pole and came up with a great flapping hornpout, nearly all head and whiskers. "Welcome, Mr. Fish! Welcome, indeed!"

He knocked the creature in the head, strung a cord through its gills, and let it trail over the side to keep fresh. Then he got back to serious fishing. We were all busy presently, and Tom Wansuc and I were soon contributing our share of the take.

When it came dark, Tom lit torches in the bow and stern, and it was all kind of mysterious and magical to be floating out there in the torchlight, dropping our lines down into the black depths, and pulling up the wriggling fishes into our own dark world.

Every time Jordan got a bite, he would sing out, "Got a whale this time!"

And every time he sung out, I had to laugh. But when Tom Wansuc, without warning, whipped a prodigious great eel into the boat, wiping me right across the neck with it as he did so, my laughter gave way to near hysterics. I hooted and roared and couldn't stop till Tom threatened to sit on me.

"Reckon mebbe we should dunk him to cool him off, Tom?" said Jordan.

"Might scare the fishes," said Tom, shaking his head.

"D-don't dunk me, p-please," I said. "I'll b-be quiet, I promise."

"Guess we got 'nough fish for one night, anyhow," Jordan said. "Let's go ashore and cook some."

Well, I had done justice to pretty heavy supper, but the smell of those pout a-roastin' on the embers revived me some. I dug in and helped polish off a half-dozen of 'em, and washed 'em down with pulls at Jordan's jug of cider.

"My Lord," declared Jordan, leaning back against a tree and rubbing his belly, "that was good eatin'."

Tom took a pull at the jug, wiped his mouth on the back of his hand, and said, "Fish is always good. I like 'em better'n meat even."

I was too full to say much. It suited me right down to the ground just to sit there and listen to the men talk and watch the flickering flames as they devoured the sticks we fed 'em.

Tom and Jordan got out their pipes and set to smoking. The good smell of their 'baccy mingled with the woodsmoke and the pond smells, and I just breathed deep and thought it delicious.

"I've about decided to join up, Tom," Jordan announced, tossing another stick onto the fire to build it up now that our cooking was done.

"Have ye?"

Jordan nodded. "Colonel says he'll get me wages if I come into the militia as a volunteer. It won't be much, but it's somethin'."

"You anxious to kill Englishmen, Jordan?"

Jordan shook his head. "Not 'specially. I don't know as I want to kill anybody. Likely I won't have to. But I sure do need the money."

"Ye wouldn't fight me for money. Why fight them?"

"It's different somehow, Tom. Lord! I hope I don't have to fight, ever. But I figger I work for the Colonel. If fightin' is part of the work he's got cut out for him, I reckon it's my part to take a hand in it."

"But Jordan," said I, not a little disturbed

by the turn this talk was taking, "the British are the enemy."

"Ain't my enemy," Tom Wansuc said. "Nor Jordan's neither."

"I dunno," Jordan said. "Now that I'm a free man, I guess mebbe they are my enemy, Tom. I don't reckon a black man would stand much of a show if the British was to win this war. They ain't too strong on the notions of a man like the Colonel. Likely they'd hang him and sell me. 'Pears to me I got a stake in this war now."

"Let white men fight each other," Tom said. "You and me, we don't belong in this business."

"How d'ye think the British would use you if they was to win, Tom?" Jordan's tone was challenging. "You think that ol' king gives a damn about an Injun?"

"You think them fellers in Philadelphia or Hartford give a damn?"

"I dunno," Jordan said. "Mebbe they don't. But if the British was to come in shootin', what would you do, Tom? Welcome 'em?"

"Hide, most likely." Tom grunted out that peculiar laugh of his. Then he said, "I guess this is my land more than anybody's. My people were here long before any whites — or blacks, either. It was whites killed us off and stole our land, and learned us about rum, cussing and the Holy Bible. I ain't lookin' to die for 'em, Jordan. That's so. But if the Reg'lars was to come, I guess mebbe I'd get my gun and pop at a few. It was Englishmen pulled my people down. Be good to get a crack at 'em on that account. 'Sides, how else can an Injun get to shoot himself some whites and not get hanged for it?"

I tell ye, it made my blood run cold to hear Tom talk so. I was surprised and proud to hear that Jordan would be joining up. I was surprised and scared to hear such talk from Tom.

Jordan must have sensed it, fir he said, "Tom Wansuc, you talk like a plain punkin-head. What're you tryin' to scare this child for, talkin' that way? You never shot nothin' fiercer than a bunny rabbit in your whole life, and here you are runnin' on like some kind of Mohawk or somethin'."

"Pequots are fierce enough, Jordan. You said so yourself."

"Fierce? Pooh! You wouldn't frighten a baby if ye was to put on paint and feathers."

"You frightened, Billy?" asked Tom, turning to me.

"Some." I was, too. It wasn't comfortable sitting there in my pale skin and listening to Tom run down whites so.

"There! See, Jordan, I frightened Billy

Latham, and he ain't a baby."

"Nossir, he sure ain't. But he don't know you the way I do. Billy, I have seen this here savage cry real tears over a bird that broke its wing, and once when —"

"You hush, Jordan!" Tom sounded mad, and I was all in a sweat for fear he'd tackle Jordan.

"Hush your own self," replied Jordan, laughing. "Or I'll tell Billy of the time you fished that poor gal out'n the river, when she'd wandered off from her ma and fallen in."

"Did ye, Tom?" said I, all fired up with interest.

"He did, certain," Jordan crowed. "And when her pa tried to give him a reward, why, this big fierce white-hatin' Injun — Wuff! Tom! What in — ?"

Tom Wansuc had plainly had enough. He picked up a fish, a pickerel it was, and swinging it by the tail, he whacked Jordan right across the skull with it. "I told you hush, you black rascal!" Tom cried, letting fly with his curious weapon again. "You hush now, or I'll wear you out with this fish."

"Ho!" cried Jordan, leaping to his feet. "You come on and try, you red devil. We'll see who gets wore out, I guess."

Well, I didn't know whether to laugh or cry, mainly because I couldn't be sure they weren't in earnest. But those two great fellows armed themselves with two fish apiece, and they went at it, thrashing and flailing and rolling around in the dirt like two boys in a schoolyard. Ye couldn't tell who was getting the worst of it, but both were catching it pretty warm. Again and again, I could hear the wet slap of a fish strike home. Sometimes Jordan was on top and sometimes Tom was, and they looked like they meant to use those fish right down to their skeletons. There was a good deal of grunting and cussing and cries of, "Take that!" and, "Oh, ye will, will ye?" And all the while that slapping kept up like the rattle of muskets from far off.

I was certain somebody was bound to be killed, whether they were in earnest or not. And that got me so upset and scared that I ran to the boat, caught up the bailer, filled it with water, then ran back and dumped it over 'em, the way ye do in breaking up a dogfight.

"Whoosh!" cried Jordan, breaking away and leaping to his feet. He'd been on top at the moment, and so caught the worst of it. But Tom got damped down some, too, and he came up sputtering. The pair of 'em looked at each other, then they glared at me standing there with the bailer in my hand.

"White folks," Tom said.

Jordan offered him his hand and said solemnly, "Tom, I hope I may die if I ever argue with you about whites again. Even the little ones got no morals. Let's get him!"

Afore I knew what they were about, I felt myself being lifted clean off the ground and rushed on down to the pond. "Help!" I cried. "Murder!"

"Murder it is," said Jordan, cheerfully. "Take his left leg, Tom."

"Got um."

And those two big villains went and soaked my head in the pond! I came up spouting water and choking and gasping and thinking I must surely die. But they bundled me back to the fire, laughing like loons, and rolled me in a blanket till I was more than half dry.

I guess I looked pretty foolish. The pair of 'em couldn't stop laughing to save their souls. Even Tom let out a couple of real "ha-ha's," which was saying a lot for him.

"Oh, Billy," cried Jordan, just hugging himself with glee, "I don't know when I've had so much fun!"

"Fun?" I cried, still wrathful. "Ye call it fun for two hulking men to try and drown a mere boy?"

"Mere?" said Jordan. "D'ye hear that, Tom? Mere. I guess a boy that tries to drown two hulkin' men ain't *mere,* exactly."

"Guess not," Tom said. "You should join up, if anybody should. You ain't a boy, you're a wildcat."

Well, that mollified me some. I mean, being called a wildcat by a tough fighter like Tom Wansuc meant something. I guess it was worth a dunking to have him call me that. But I didn't tell them that. I knew better by now.

Jordan guessed I was over my mad. He put his arm around my shoulder and said, "We still friends, ain't we, Billy?"

I had to grin. "I guess so, Jordan. But my mother ain't goin' to love ye any better when she catches sight of these clothes."

Jordan rolled his eyes as if in terror. "Ye won't tell on us, will ye, Billy? I'm mighty scared o' your mother. She'd lay me out with a skillet and not wait for no explanations."

That got me to giggling. I could just see Mother chasing Jordan through the town, hitching up her skirts with one hand and slinging her skillet with the other.

"Whew!" said Jordan. "I guess we're saved, Tom. Looks like Billy Latham's got over his mad."

"Good thing," Tom said. "I'd rather fight ten Englishmen than one Latham. They're fiercer even than Pequots."

It was about the best evening I ever hope to have. But it was getting dreadful late. We broke up the fire and slung the burning brands high into the air, arcing like meteors against the night sky, to *skoosh* out in the rippling water of the pond. Then we stumbled our way back to the wagon, loaded on the boat, and headed back through the woods for home.

To this day, I don't know what put it into my head. It might have been just the accumulation of all that foolishness. Then again, it may have been the Devil. However it was, as we neared the village, I said, "Say, Tom, what'll ye take for that eel?"

"What I can get," said Tom, eyeing the still wriggling creature.

An eel, ye see, takes a lot of killing. I have known eels to be chopped up, skinned and ready for the pan and still wriggle. I have seen 'em wriggle in the pan. I don't care to speculate on what they do after they're et. They say a cat has nine lives, and I don't doubt it. But an eel hangs on its one life more tenaciously than any other creature God ever made.

"I'll give ye my mouth-organ for it," I said.

Tom sniffed. "I don't fancy it," he said. "But if you are so partial to eels, I'll trade him off for two of your perch."

"Done," said I, and the trade was made.

When Jordan reined in before my house, there wasn't a light showing. I jumped down, whispered good night, and slipped into the house. I stole through to the kitchen and set my fish in a tub to keep. Then, taking a sure grip on my eel, I tip-toed up the stairs and turned down the hall towards Lucy's room. I halted outside her door, listening as hard as I could. Nothing. Not a sound. Softly, ever softly, I pushed her door ajar. It was dark as the Pit and stiller than a tomb. I could just about make out the sound of her breathing. One step, two, three, and I was standing right by her bed. Gently, ever so gently, I lifted a corner of the coverlet, and I tucked Mr. Eel in for the night.

Then I lit out for the garret, shucked off my clothes and hopped into bed.

I lay there snickering to myself, waiting for the fun to start. And I waited. Nothing. I began to feel uneasy, and for the first time it crossed my mind that I was headed for trouble. If Lucy was to react the way I'd hoped she would, it would surely rouse the house. There'd be no doubt as to who did it, and there was no doubt in my own mind as to what the consequences would be.

I didn't dare go back and try to retrieve my eel. Yet I didn't relish the thought of a visit from Father, either. I was between a rock and a hard place, and I didn't feel so clever as I had a few moments before.

Still nothing. Maybe the eel had died. It didn't seem likely. He was lively enough when I tucked him in. I couldn't fathom it for the life of me.

Between waiting for the screeching to commence and dreading the midnight visit from Father that must surely follow, I couldn't lie easy. But somewhere in the small hours, sleep must have overtaken me, for the next thing I knew the sunlight was streaming in at my window.

It was awful late, and I was tired and achey and in no mood to leave my bed. But there was nothing for it but to go down and face the family. I dragged my carcass out of bed, pulled on my breeches, and went on down the stairs like a condemned man going to the gallows.

CHAPTER IX

I walked into that kitchen like a man carrying a lighted torch into a powderhouse. But Father only looked up from his plate and said, "Better hurry, Will. We don't want to be late."

"N-No, Sir."

I slid into my place and helped myself to a bowl of mush.

" 'Mornin', Billy," said Lucy, just as nice as pie. "Did ye have any luck last night?"

"Um. Why, yes. Yes, we did."

"That's nice."

Mother came in with a platter of sausages and fried eggs. "Good mornin', Billy," said she, cheerful and bright. "Pass your plate and I'll dish ye out some vittles."

I couldn't understand it. I knew I had put that eel in Lucy's bed. I couldn't have dreamed it. Or could I? No, that was foolish. I'd had dreams that were terribly real and terribly strange, but I never dreamed such a thing as that.

I sat there, piling the food into my face and going over the whole evening in my mind. Tom had caught an eel. I had traded off a couple of perch for it. I had carried it wriggling and writhing up the stairs. I had gone into Lucy's room, and I had surely put it into her bed. I knew I had. And yet —"

" 'bout finished, Will?" Father said, getting to his feet.

"Um," I grunted, my mouth full of grub. I drained off a mug of cider, scooped up a slab of pie, and hurried off with Father to the Fort.

First to greet us was Ensign Ebenezer Avery. We said our good mornings, then he eyed me with an odd sort of look and said, "Ye're lookin' uncommon handsome this mornin', Billy."

"Us Lathams always was long on looks," said Father grinning wide. "A mite shy on brains, mebbe, but handsome."

Ensign Avery grunted. "Handsome is as handsome does, Cap'n, so I allus say."

"I have heard ye say it more than once," Father said.

"Truth bears repeatin'," the ensign said, with a sniff.

Father liked Ensign Avery. Of course, they'd known each other all their lives, and had practically grown up together. But Father often said there was no one he took more pleasure in joshing than Ebenezer Avery, because Avery seemed never to be certain if he was being joshed or not. He wasn't without humor, though, and he was a brave man, and handy, too.

"Better get along to your chores, Will," Father said, giving me a dig in the ribs. "It's goin' to be a warm day."

I made tracks for the well, and ran into Barney Kinne, the minister's son. "How do, Barney?" said I, polite as ye please.

"We-ll," drawled Barney, "don't we look smart this morning? Mighty handsome, Billy, mighty handsome."

And he walked off shaking his head.

I began to think the whole world had gone daft.

I lowered my bucket and was drawing it up when along came Corporal Andrew Billings. He walked by with a cheery "How do," then stopped, turned and came back. "Billy," he said, "Ye're gettin' to be a reg'lar macaroni."

"Huh?" said I, with considerable brilliance.

"Yessir," he said, "a reg'lar macaroni. Every gal in town'll be settin' her cap for you."

And off he went, whistling merrily.

I hauled my bucket up, convinced that lunacy had broken out among the men. Something was up. I didn't know what, and I didn't know why, but it was ripening fast and getting higher than a dead cat in July.

My first stop was over to the parapet where Captain Youngs Ledyard, nephew to the Colonel and son to the Squire, was drilling the men in loading and sighting the big guns. I scaled the ladder and set my bucket down, sloshing a good bit over my toes as I did so.

"Here's the water, Cap'n," said I.

"Thank ye, Billy," he said. And I turned to go. "Billy!"

"Sir?" I could see some of the men were grinning and whispering among themselves. I grinned, too, not knowing why, but not wanting to seem out of it.

Captain Ledyard walked up to me, frowning. He was always a serious-minded young man, very conscious of his position in the town, and burdened beyond his years with a sense of the responsibilities that went with it. Not that he was stuffy, mind ye, but grave as a deacon and sober as a judge.

"Billy," said he, looking down on me sternly, "you realize this Fort is not a playground."

"Yes, Sir," said I, the grin fading from my face.

"It may be a lark for you to come here and hang about every day, but I must remind you that we are men here, doing men's work. We've no time for foolishness."

I didn't appreciate that about my hanging about. That rankled, because I did work, and blamed hard, too. But I was so puzzled by the man's tone and his evident displeasure that I let the slander pass unchallenged and just gaped at him, completely bewildered.

"If you have an explanation for your appearance this morning, I am prepared to hear it," he said, folding his arms across his breast and fixing me with a cold blue eye.

"Cap'n Ledyard, excuse me, but I don't understand —"

I scratched my head — Je-rusalem!

My fingers touched something mighty strange. I gave a yank, and pulled off the prettiest pink ribbon ye ever saw.

Well, I was some staggered, I promise ye. I stood there gawking at it as if it were some kind of marvel, like a white crow or a six-legged sheep. The captain must have realized then that I was the victim and not the joker, for his tone softened and the ghost of a smile flitted across his lips. "I think," he said, "I think you will want to remove all of them, Billy. They really do not become you."

"All of 'em!"

My fingers flew to my head and felt my hair all over. Sweet Moses! There must have been a half-dozen bows knotted there. I tore at 'em, I can tell ye, yanking 'em out and flinging 'em to the ground, reds and yellows and pinks and pale blues. I guess my face must have turned every one of those colors, too. I could hear the men laughing, and I could feel the fire of mortification go crackling all along my spine. I never felt so cheap and foolish in all my days. I just wished the ground would open up and swallow me. I didn't see how I could ever look any of those men in the face again.

To give the captain his due, he turned on the men and ordered 'em to hush up. Then he said to me, "Don't feel too bad, Billy. They've had their laugh and now it's over. By tomorrow, it'll all be forgot."

I was so mortified I couldn't speak. The tears were stinging my eyelids, and there was a lump the size of a cannonball in my throat. I just turned and ran, not knowing or caring where, just bent on clearing out so I'd never have to face any of 'em again. Two or three called out as I went smoking by 'em, but I just kept my head down and my heels flying, making for the gate at top speed. I'd have gone, too, and probably not stopped running till I was into Rhode Island, but from out of nowhere a strong hand flew, caught me by the shoulder and pulled me to a sudden halt.

"Goin' somewhere, Will?"

It was Father.

I couldn't bear to look at him, and I didn't dare say what I was feeling. He had known. He had let me walk out among those men looking like — like a blamed fool. In ribbons! I'd never forgive him if I was to live to be a hundred.

"The well is over that way, Will," he said. "The men'll be wantin' their water."

"I can't do it," I muttered, looking down at my toes.

"What d'ye mean, Will?"

I looked up then, my eyes swimming, my face all red with shame and anger. "I can't face 'em," I said. "They're all laughin' at me. You-you let Lucy make a fool of me, and I can't bear it, and I won't."

Father cupped his hand under my chin and held my eyes with his. "Will," he said, "when it comes down to who made a fool of you, I reckon you were ahead of Lucy by about a mile. She gave ye a dose of your own medicine; now we'll see if ye're man enough to swaller it.

"You may go if ye wish, boy. I'll not force ye to stay against your will. But I'd be sorry to think that a son o' mine wasn't man enough to stand up to a serving of humble pie, especially when he had it comin' to him.

"It's up to you, Will. D'ye mean to run off with your tail between your legs, or will ye stay here with the men?"

I mopped at my eyes and wiped my nose on my sleeve, feeling more ashamed of my tears than I'd been of those plaguey ribbons. I was glad none of the men could see me blubbering.

"Well, boy?"

I nodded. "I'll stay, Father," I said, my voice croaky as a bullfrog's.

"Thought ye might," he said, pulling my ears goodnaturedly. "Now get along about your work."

It was a long day, about the longest I'd ever put in. I imagined that everybody was laughing at me, and some were, no doubt. The only thing that sustained me was the thought of vengeance. I purely hated Lucy that day, and there wasn't a thing too mean to consider doing to her. On the contrary, I couldn't think of anything mean enough. And I thought of plenty. Every time I dropped that bucket down into the well, I'd think of what a splash Lucy would make if I was to drop her in. And every time a man walked past toting a musket or a pike, the blood-thirstiest kind of notions would spring up in my brain. I finally concluded that the only revenge that would even come close to being satisfactory would be to stuff her in a cannon and shoot her clear across the Thames. Then they could dispatch a search party to round up the pieces. By the time they collected enough to pray over, I would be in China or the Azores. Let 'em come after me, if they thought her worth the bother. I'd go to the gallows content, and drop through the trap with a smile.

The day did end, finally. They all do, however long they seem. And Father and I hiked along home to supper. We were about halfway there when Father broke the silence that was growing up between us.

"Hard day, wasn't it, Will?"

"Awful," I said.

"Guess you're of a mind to about kill Lucy."

I shot him a sidewise glance, but there was nothing in his expression to make me cautious. So I said, "I thought about it."

Father nodded. "Doesn't surprise me any. But, really, Will, you ought to feel obliged to your sister."

"Obliged!" I could feel the anger heating up in my gizzard. "After what she done?"

Father draped an arm across my shoulder. "She spared ye worse, boy, I promise ye. You value comin' to the Fort every day, don't ye?"

"Yes, Sir."

"Well," he said, "if it hadn't a-been for Lucy, you'd have lost that. When I heard about your foolishness of last night, I was bound you should be punished for it. And the only fit punishment I could think of was to forbid ye to come to the Fort anymore."

I came near to swallowing my tongue.

"Yessir," Father went on, "I was intent on that very thing. But Lucy said, 'twas only mischief, and she didn't want for ye to suffer unduly. She calc'lated she'd had her revenge, and she asked that I let that suffice.

"I thought it over, and it seemed to me that what she'd done was about right. Nonsense for nonsense, as ye might say. But if it hadn't a-been for her puttin' her oar in, you'd be unemployed today, and barred from the Fort hereafter."

That gave me quite enough to think about the rest of the way home.

I didn't say much all through supper. Nor did Lucy. Mercifully, it seemed that all at home were of a mind to let the matter rest, and I was thankful. When I found out how near I'd come to losing my situation, I went all weak in the knees; and somehow the shame I'd felt over those cussed ribbons didn't seem so all-fired dreadful now. Compared to being barred from the Fort, it didn't amount to shucks. If someone had told me that forenoon that I'd be feeling grateful to Lucy before sundown, I'd have set him down for a fool and worse. But there it was. She'd saved my bacon, and I reckoned that evened things between us.

After supper, Lucy announced that she was taking the scraps out to the hog. I said, "Let me give ye a hand with that, Lucy."

She looked at me with considerable suspicion, thinking, no doubt, that I had some notions of tripping her up in the mud or maybe having a little "accident" at the horse trough. But whatever else she may have been, Lucy was no coward. She gave me a little toss of her head and said, "Come along then, if ye've a mind to."

I took the pail and walked with her out to the sty. I served the old tusker his dinner and then, leaning on the fence and pretending to watch him eat, I said, "Lucy, when did ye find it?"

She knew what I meant and, unlike a grownup, she answered directly. "I was awake when you came in."

"And ye didn't yip?" I was struck with wonder.

"Well, I wanted to, right enough. Ugh!" She shuddered from head to toe. "But I wasn't about to give you the satisfaction. Soon as you quit my room, I jumped out of bed, and I piled everything I could find on top of that — that serpent. Then I settled down in my chair and waited."

"Waited?"

"Till I was pretty certain you had to be

asleep. That gave me plenty of time to form my plan. And the thinking helped to keep me awake — that, and my dread of that viper."

" 'Twasn't a viper, Lucy. Only an eel."

"It's all the same to me, thank'ee. I don't fancy anything that don't have legs." She grinned, and for the first time it struck me that my sister was going to be pretty. She had blue eyes, like Father, and chestnut hair, like Mother. And she was beginning to fill out some, and take on the look of a young woman. I felt a little awed and some startled. It never occurred to me that my skinny, freckle-faced arch-enemy was anything other than a knobby-kneed pest.

"Anyway," Lucy went on, "when I thought of ribbons, I knew I'd hit on the very thing. I stole down the hall and up the steps to your room. You were sleepin' like a dead man. I could have cut your hair all off, if I'd have had a mind to. For a boy with a conscience as burdened as yours must be, you do sleep soundly.

"A good thing, too. For I was able to get downstairs before you and let the family in on the plot. They all agreed to keep mum, and well, you know the rest, I guess."

"Guess so," I said. "And I know, too, that ye put in a word for me with Father."

Lucy sniffed. "Oh, that. Well, I guess I can

settle my own scores without any help from Father. Although I did ask him to get that — that thing out of my bed. I couldn't bear to even think of handling it."

"Well, all the same, I'm beholden to ye," I said, and it cost me something to say so, though not as much as I'd expected.

"Guess we'd better get back to the house," Lucy said.

I picked up the pail and we started back.

"Lucy?"

"What?"

"We even?"

"I guess so." She smiled at me, quite friendly. "Was it bad for you at the Fort today?"

"Pretty bad. I — I almost cut and run."

"I guess it was pretty mean of me to deck you out like that."

"Well, it was mean of me to put that eel in your bed."

Lucy sighed. "I guess we are just two mean Lathams, Billy. I wonder if there is any hope for us at all."

"Might be," I said, "if we was to stick together."

"Well, let's" she said, and stuck out her hand. I shook it, not feeling the least bit foolish. I figured a sister with enough grit not to screech when you put an eel in her bed was a sister to be proud of.

I figured, too, that a boy with a sister smart enough to pull off a stunt like the one Lucy had pulled on me would be wise to make peace and bury the hatchet. Otherwise, there was just no telling what she might do next.

CHAPTER X

With the truce between Lucy and me, life was duller, but safer. It took some getting used to, our being polite and friendly to one another. When it became unbearable, I would whisper, "Serpent!" And Lucy would fire back, "Ribbons!" And we'd both laugh and feel easy.

The teasing from the men at the Fort eased up gradually. I found that if I laughed along with 'em, it relieved the sting considerably, too. They were kept so busy that they hadn't much time for foolishness. Colonel Ledyard worked 'em hard. Rumors rode into town on every breeze. There was talk of Washington's attacking New York; of Clinton's invading New England; of retaliation against New London for the taking of the *Hannah*; of just about every kind of calamity short of Judgment Day.

Captain Amos Stanton, on furlough from the Continental Army, was a frequent visitor to the Fort. He was a great bear of a man, as tall at least as Jordan, and heavier. He'd fought in any number of battles since the very beginning of the war, and I think Ledyard himself was a little in awe of him. I noticed that the Colonel spent a good deal of time listening to Stanton and in showing him around the Fort, getting his opinion of our strength and our capabilities.

I'm proud to say the Colonel took the trouble to introduce me to Captain Stanton.

"This is Will Latham's boy, Amos," he said. "He makes himself useful hereabouts, and we all set considerable store by him."

My hand was all but swallowed up in Stanton's huge paw. I think I should have had to climb a tree to greet him properly. As it was, I had to crane my neck to meet his eyes with mine.

"If ye turn out to be the man your father is, ye'll be welcome to fight alongside me anytime," Stanton said.

"I mean to be like him," I said.

"Do that," said he, "and ye need never feel ashamed to look any man in the face."

My fingers were cramped for two days afterwards, but I shall always be glad that I got to shake hands with Amos Stanton. He was the most man I ever set eyes on, and among the bravest. Seeing him stalking about the Fort was a tonic. Somehow you knew that the British must lose when you were standing in the shadow of a man like that.

Jordan was at the Fort daily now, having

signed on as a volunteer — not, as he emphasized again, to kill Reg'lars, but to look after his Colonel. And Tom Wansuc, to my surprise, turned up, too. He allowed that someone would have to look after "that fool Jordan" while he was looking after Ledyard, or he'd go and get himself killed for certain. Jordan only grinned and said Tom was really set on lifting hair, and that it was all lies about wanting to look after him.

"That ain't so," Tom said. "Fact is, you never paid me the five shillin's I lent ye last winter. If you was to die, I'd never get my money. I'm stickin' by ye to protect my interests."

It was good to have Tom and Jordan about. Of course, they were not blessed with many idle moments. They had to learn the care and feeding of the big guns, and they had to drill, too, although Jordan had only an old whaling lance for a weapon. He could not afford a musket, and there were precious few around to buy anyway.

But, busy as they were, and busy as I was myself, it was a rare day that didn't afford me a chance to talk with one or the other, or both. I found myself growing more at ease with Tom Wansuc. It got so I really looked forward to seeing him. He was not an easy man to know, and I had misread him somewhat because of the nature of our first meeting. But once I learned to let him open up at his own rate and in his own time, why, I found him almost as easy to talk with as Jordan.

Jordan, I think, had the heart of a child. Not that he was soft or foolish; far from it. But his was a sunny spirit, genial and warm. He had pride; his refusal to perform for Colonel Harris had proved that; but there was nothing stiff or stand-offish about him. Knowing him and liking him was easy as breathing, and as natural.

Tom, though, had a kind of shell. He could be standing right next to ye, and yet be as far off as China. He didn't give himself away, and he took his own sweet time about responding to another's proffers of friendship. Indeed, I'd have to say that, so far as I know, Jordan was the only real friend Tom had. Jordan could do or say just about anything, no matter how outrageous, and Tom would only smile. But I would not have given a penny for the chances of another man who tried such stuff on Tom Wansuc. Once, and only once, Sergeant Ezekial Bailey, a good-natured man but a poor judge of character, tried to jolly Tom. He came walking up one day while Tom was talking with Jordan and me, whacked Tom on the back and said, "Why ain't ye wearin' your feathers, Chief?"

Slowly, very slowly, Tom turned around, his face like a block of Stony Creek granite, his eyes like agates, shining and hard. He just stared into Bailey's face till the poor man was utterly discomposed, then he turned back to us and resumed talking as though Sergeant Bailey wasn't even there. Bailey slunk off, feeling pretty cheap. I felt bad for him, for I knew he'd meant no harm; but I was glad I wasn't walking in his shoes just then.

Whether it was because of Jordan, or just because he was getting used to my being around, Tom seemed to warm to me. I took care never to push myself on him, and I minded my tongue with uncommon caution when he was about; yet I did like him, and I knew he liked me, because if he hadn't, he wouldn't have troubled himself to hide the fact. Knowing that gave me some measure of confidence in approaching him, and ye had to have that with him.

One noon, late in August, I came upon Tom taking his ease in the shade of the barracks. He was just polishing off the last of his luncheon, so I took an apple from my pocket and lighted alongside him on the sunburnt grass.

"How do, Billy?" he said. "You hidin' from work?"

"I'd like to," said I. "It sure is hot today."

"Hot enough," Tom allowed. "Seen Jordan?"

"He's run into luck. The Colonel's sent him to Fort Trumbull with a message for Captain Shapley."

"Good day to be on the river," Tom said. "Or in it."

"Ay-uh. I was hopin' I could go with him, but the way you men are lappin' up water today, I can't be spared. Damn it."

Tom cocked a quizzical eye at me. "When did you start cussin', boy?"

"This summer."

"Well, stop it. It don't become you."

I felt sheepish. Fact is, I'd heard more brisk language that summer than I'd ever heard before. I thought it manly, and I felt more soldierly somehow when I employed it. Boylike, I tried to defend myself by saying, "You cuss, Tom. I've heard you."

Tom favored me with a freezing look and said, "If I was to swaller a toad, would you do it, too?"

"No."

"Well, then."

I can't say that I gave up cussing altogether, but since that day I have never really been able to enjoy it.

Tom stretched cat-fashion and got to his

feet. "Guess we'll see no more of Jordan this day," he said, hitching up his breeches.

"Why not?"

"He's in New London, ain't he? Guess he wouldn't miss a chance to see his woman."

"You know about Sally?"

"Me and Jordan's friends, ain't we?"

I didn't feel jealous, exactly; only a little humbled by the realization that Tom had a claim on Jordan, too, and was at least as informed as I was about Jordan's private business.

"Have you met her?" I asked.

"I have. You?"

"Ay-uh."

Tom nodded. "She's a mighty good woman, that Sally. Jordan's lucky. Ain't many like her."

It struck me as strange at the time. Tom had set me down hard just now for cussing, yet he called Sally a good woman. Surely he knew she was carrying Jordan's baby, and surely he knew she wasn't Jordan's wife. Not yet, anyway. It was beyond me. The only way I could figure it was that Tom, not being a Christian, didn't see the sinfulness of the thing. Yet he seemed to know the wrong in cussing. I couldn't square it, but it didn't seem prudent to air my doubts, and I judged it wasn't my place to try to instruct him, so I just said, "She is mighty pretty."

Tom grunted. "More'n that, I reckon." He frowned down on me, seeming to wrestle with his thoughts. Then he said, "You know about the baby?"

I nodded.

"That worries me, Billy Latham," he said. "It purely worries me."

"Me, too."

"Jordan ain't got fifty dollars to his name. How he expects to buy Sally free afore she's found out, I just can't figger."

"I mean to give him my savings," I said.

Tom favored me with one of his rare smiles. "You'll do, boy," he said.

We Yankees are not given to gushing. But alongside an Injun, we seem as effusive as the French. For Tom Wansuc to say, "You'll do" was equal to a speech from Patrick Henry or a whole book by Tom Paine. I knew what he meant, and I felt honored.

"Thing is," he went on, "Jordan won't take your money."

"Why not?"

Tom shrugged. "He won't take mine. He knows I got no use for it. I got a house, a garden patch and a canoe. Plenty of fish in the river, game in the woods. I don't need money. I told Jordan he could pay me back in thirty, forty years, for all I care. But he said no."

"But that's foolish."

"That's Jordan." Tom shook his head. "I got enough to buy Sally free twice over, but he means to do it himself. Don't ask me how. Rate he's goin', she'll be a grandma afore he's got enough cash laid by."

"Can't ye make him take it, Tom?"

Tom gave me an odd look. "Ye're talkin' to the wrong Pequot," he said.

He went back to his labors then, leaving me lowspirited and uneasy. True, it was Jordan's problem, not mine; but I liked him. And I liked Sally. If they were going to Hell, as I thought likely, it seemed to me that they ought at least have some happiness whilst they were among the living. I don't know what Mr. Kinne would have made of my reasoning, but that's how I felt. I couldn't help it.

I kept moving, and I kept busy, but all that long afternoon I had Jordan on my mind. As I lowered my bucket for the hundredth time in the course of that sweltering day, I was startled half out of my skin to hear his voice behind me:

"Give me a drink, Billy. I'm dry as a salt mackerel."

"Jordan. You're back!"

He didn't say anything to that, only took

the dipper and scooped up some water, but his hand shook so that he spilled about half of it before he could get the dipper to his lips. His face was streaked with sweat and dust, and his ordinarily glistening black skin looked faded, almost gray. His eyes, when at last he lowered the dipper and looked at me, showed mingled anger and pain.

"Wh-what's the matter, Jordan? What's wrong?"

"He drove me off." The words came out as though bitten off one by one.

"Who?"

"Colonel Harris." Jordan took another dipperful, sucked up the water noisily, sloshed it around in his mouth and jetted it out onto the ground. He stood there, looking off towards New London, his face grim and hard. "He drove me off, boy. He shamed me in front of her."

I didn't know what to say. To me, Jordan was a champion, a giant, all that was strong and noble and good. I couldn't bear to look at him, to see the hurt and humiliation in his face. I knew he could have broken Colonel Harris across his knee like a stick of kindling, and I couldn't understand why he had allowed himself to be chased off like a stray dog.

"How — how could ye let him do it to you, Jordan?" I said.

"Let him?" Jordan spat into the yellowing grass. "He had a musket, boy. I was standin' with my back to him, out by the barn, talkin' with Sally. Next thing I knew, I felt somethin' hard in the small of my back. I turned around, and that damned musket was pointed right at my middle.

" 'Get out o' here, Nigger,' he said. 'And don't never come back. If I catch you around here again, I'll shoot first and talk afterwards.'

"I couldn't do nothing. And I wouldn't say nothin'. I didn't want Sally punished on account of me. So I just — slunk off." Jordan rubbed his face with both hands. "I was shamed, Billy. I was the most shamed I ever was in my whole life."

"He had a weapon, Jordan. There was nothin' ye could do."

"That's it. That's what riles me so," said Jordan, his jaws clenched tight. "There was nothin' I could do."

Someone, Luke Perkins, I think it was, sung out from the parapet, "Hey, Billy! The well gone dry?"

"Comin'!" I yelled. Then I said, "I got to go, Jordan."

"Go 'long, Billy," he said. "I ain't in a mood for talkin' anyway."

I hustled along up to the parapet with my bucket; then, taking a roundabout course, I caught up with Tom Wansuc and told him what had happened. He didn't seem surprised, only nodded and said, "It was bound to happen. You go along. I'll see to Jordan."

I can recall little more of that afternoon. I know I was about as unhappy as I could ever remember being. I wanted to see Jordan, and yet I didn't. There wasn't a thing I could say or do that would be of any comfort to him, and it was certainly no comfort to me to see him so wounded and so far beyond my power to help.

That evening, I was so jumpy that I could hardly stand my own company. I couldn't sit still and I couldn't shake off the blue devils that had laid hold of me. The house seemed to be closing in on me, and just the voices of the family running on about ordinary things grated on my ears like the sound of chains being dragged over a rough stone floor.

Father had gone out. Mother and the gals were making a great clatter in the kitchen, and jabbering away like a flock of grackles. Luke was getting a tooth, and he was squalling so that it would drive a body mad to listen to it another minute. I had to get out into the air or bust.

Deliverance came in the person of Deborah Ledyard. Just as I was composing an impassioned plea for liberty — my own — in my head, to persuade Mother to let me loose for an hour or two, Miss Deborah came clumping up the steps, all hot and out of breath, to announce the imminent arrival of a new baby at her house. "Ma's took awful bad with her pains," she said. "She says her time's come."

Mother would have made a capital minuteman. She set down the plate she was scraping, switched aprons, and was out the back door like a shot. Now we were a house without a government. And I didn't waste my opportunity.

"Mary," said I, to my eldest sister, "I have a notion to go see if there are any fish biting down to the river."

"And to go swimmin', too, I expect." Mary was ever so much pleasanter since she'd been spoken for, and she was less inclined now to play the role of deputy-mother.

"It is a middlin' warm evenin'," I said.

"Go along, Billy," she said. "Only don't drown yourself, and don't be out all night. I'll square things with Father when he comes in."

"Boys have all the fun," said Lucy, up to her elbows in dishwater.

"Never mind, Lucy," I said. "I'll bring ye back a nice fat eel to make it up to ye."

A sodden dishrag whizzed past my ear and

hit the wall with a dull damp thud. That cheered me up considerably, and I was more than half tempted to sling it back at her, but I only put out my tongue at her and skinned out into the golden twilight.

Lord, it was good to breathe again! I began to think I might be willing to try living a while longer. The river beckoned, and I scuffed along the winding dirt road, just enjoying the feel of the warm dust between my toes and the light breeze stirring my hair. I came at last to the ferry slip and, taking advantage of some convenient greenery, I shed my clothes and dived into the coolish salt water. Oh, it felt good!

I paddled out a ways, then rolled over and floated on my back, just a-bobbing on the wavelets and looking up in wonder at the fading colors in the sky. In after years, when I heard from travellers of mineral springs and medicinal waters, I couldn't help but think that if ever I was taken sick, I know where I'd go. I'd just drag my bones to the bank of the Thames. A swim in those blue waters would be all the cure I'd need.

I didn't want to come out, not even after my finger ends began to crinkle. It was just so blessed good to be off by myself, to feel free, to swim and splash and dive like an otter at play. It was as if I'd broken off connections with the land, its people and their problems. I felt clean and strong and wild. I was for that brief time no longer a properly tamed boy from a properly tamed village, with its tame school and its tame church and its tame elders. I was own brother to the porpoise and the whale, a merboy, if ye please, half-human, half-fish; and for one fleeting, almost frightening moment, I felt an overpowering urge to lose my being in the great, endlessly rolling waters of the Atlantic, to become one with the spray and the foam.

Whether it was the gathering gloaming or the strangeness of my own thoughts, I do not know; but I was suddenly afraid, and I turned over and struck out briskly for the darkening shore. I barked my shins in scrabbling up the bank, but I did not feel the smart till long afterwards, so eager was I to get on solid ground again. The air was sultry still, but I was actually shivering as I hustled into my clothes. I wanted to see lamplight, to hear voices, and be with folks again, and renew my citizenship of Earth.

I hurried up the narrow path, unmindful of the sword grass slicing at my legs, and the gnats swarming about my ears. As I neared the top of the embankment, I halted and drew in my breath with a sharp sudden hiss. A man was standing there, motionless, a blocky figure silhouetted against a purple velvet sky.

"That you, Billy?"

My heart resumed beating. "Tom?"

"It's me. What you doin' here?"

"Takin' a swim. You out for a walk?"

Tom Wansuc offered his hand and hauled me up to the rise on which he was standing. "I've just come from Jordan," he said.

"How — how is he?"

"Not good. He's got it into his head that he's been shamed before Sally. He just sits there and vows he'll never see her no more."

"But he can't, Tom. He — he cares for her. And there's the baby coming, and —"

"Uhn. Don't you think I told him that?" Tom shook his head. "I can't budge him, Billy Latham. I'm bound to go and see what his woman can do."

"You're going — over there? To Colonel Harris's?"

"It'll be dark in another minute. I mean to paddle across and fetch her, and bring her to Jordan to see if she can't talk sense into him."

"Let me go with you."

I felt rather than saw Tom's gaze boring into me, as if he were judging the weight of a calf or a pig. Then he said, "Jordan's your friend, too. I guess it's right you should come."

Tom fixed his fingers into my shoulder and steered me back down the bank. I watched in silent astonishment as he stepped lightly over the slick and treacherous stones to where a tangle of choke-cherry and sumac grew up at the water's edge. He bent back the pliant branches with one hand, and with the other he pulled a canoe from out of the tiny inlet screened in by the trees. He stepped into his frail craft and, with a single thrust of his paddle, he drove it up alongside the bank. "Get in, Wildcat," he said.

In another minute, we were gliding across the dark water, our prow aiming straight for the New London shore.

CHAPTER XI

We stole our way through the dark and silent town, with only an occasional ray of lamplight and the faint glow of the waning moon to guide us. The night was warm, but I felt an autumn chill all along my backbone as we neared the summit of Town Hill. If I had shadowed Tom any closer, I'd have walked right over him; but I was of no mind to get separated, I promise ye.

At the top of the rise, we could just make out the earthworks of Fort Nonsense, and we could hear the measured tread of the sentries making their rounds. It gave me a good feeling to know that these men were awake and alert, and it was somehow reassuring to know that Tom and I were not the only souls abroad that night.

Tom grasped my wrist and whispered, "This way."

He slipped along through the shadows, circling Colonel Harris's house and coming up at the rear of the barn.

"Stand fast," he muttered. And he cupped his hands to his mouth and sent up the whip-poor-will call. Once, twice, a third time, then I saw a stream of light spill out into the yard as the back door swung out; a slight figure showed briefly in silhouette, then disappeared into the darkness as the door swung to. I heard Sally run lightly down the path, halt, and call softly, "Jordan?"

"Not Jordan. Tom Wansuc."

"Oh, Tom!" Sally drew near. "Did Jordan send you?"

"No. We came on his account."

Then Sally noticed me, lurking back of Tom. "Billy Latham, that you?"

"Ay-uh," I said. "How do, Sally?"

"Shh. Talk low," Tom cautioned. "Sally, Jordan's awful unhappy. He feels shamed and sick in his heart. Will ye come talk to him?"

Sally didn't hesitate a second. "I'll come," she said. "Only I must wait till Mistress is gone to bed."

"She goin' soon?"

"Very soon now. You wait here, Tom. I'll come to you quick as I can."

Tom grunted. "We'll wait," he said.

Sally flew back to the house, and Tom and I hunkered down to wait. We were situated comfortably enough, I guess. Leastways we were warm and dry. But I couldn't seem to lose the butterflies that were flapping around in my innards, and every minute dragged along as if anchored fore and aft. Tom didn't talk, and I guessed he wanted nothing but a lot of silence from me. I scrunched in the grass and leaned my back against the barn and tried to compose myself to sweat it out.

Now and then a mosquito helped himself to about a quart of my blood, and various kinds of winged things hummed by in the dark, making me itch just to hear 'em. Lightning bugs showed their lanterns in the high grass, and I could heat bats squeaking overhead. That made my skin crawl. I knew there was nothing a bat liked better than to tangle himself up in a body's hair, and I doubted I could keep mum if that happened. I knew I mustn't peep, but there is only so much that flesh can stand. If a bat was to light on my head, it would be all up with me.

My knees were beginning to ache, and I itched where I couldn't reach. The more I tried not to notice, the worse it got. And to add to my misery, there came on a sudden and most urgent need to make water. I did my best to ignore it, to think about other things, but it wasn't any use. I had to relieve myself or bust.

"Tom," I whispered. "Tom?"

"Uhn."

"Tom, I got to piss."

"Can't it keep?"

"No!"

"Get 'round to the far side, then," he whispered, "and keep quiet."

I got to my feet and stumbled off, my legs all pins and needles. I did what I had to do, and felt considerably better. But the feeling didn't last, for as I came around to the back again, I heard close by a low, menacing growl that turned my blood to slush. It sounded so mean and so threatening that I reckoned it had to be a bear or a wolf, at least. But it was only a hound. I say "only," but it was just about as bad as if it had been a bear. All we needed was to have that fool dog set up a holler.

I just froze, not sure of the creature's intentions. He was as uncertain of mine, I guess, for he circled around me, sniffing at my ankles as though trying to decide which one was the tastier. I tried clicking my tongue at him, but my mouth was so dry that I made poor work of it. My confidence was draining fast. If I couldn't keep still with a bat in my hair, what would I do with a sixty pound dog fastened to my leg? I'd heard about the tale of the Spartan boy with the wolf in his bosom, and how he kept mum though the varmint chewed right through to his vitals. But I was no Spartan, only a scared little Yankee. And I knew that I was bound to sing out at the first bite.

Then, mercifully, I heard a whisper. "Billy! Come on!"

"I can't," I whispered back. It was a pretty loud whisper, and pretty desperate, too. On hearing me, that dog took up growling again, more seriously now, as though he'd made up his mind which leg to take off.

"What's that?" Tom hissed.

"D-dog!"

Tom's moccasins whispered over the grass, and in an instant he had that animal by the scruff of the neck. Speaking low, but forceful, he said something to it in his own language. That hound went down on its belly just as meek as a lamb and wagged its tail in a most neighborly fashion. Tom roughed up its fur some, then said, "Let's slide, Billy. Sally's come."

The three of us faded out of there stealthy as stoats, Sally clutching my hand the whole of the way back down to the river. There wasn't any talk till we'd pushed off, and precious little then. Tom was not what ye'd call a talker at the best of times, and Sally, I guess, was too full of her thoughts of Jordan. As for me, I'd had about all the talk scared out of me. What little was left was damped down considerably by the thought of the reception that was likely waiting for me to home.

Tom, with a last strong thrust of his paddle, drove the canoe into the shore and held her steady while I helped Sally out. Then he shoved his craft back into her hiding place and came over to lead us up the bank. We moved alone lively up the hill to Ledyard's place and slipped around to Jordan's cabin.

"You go in," Tom told Sally. "I'll wait and take you back across when ye're ready."

"I'll wait, too," I said, as much curious to know Jordan's reaction as I was eager to see the adventure through.

"No," Tom said. "It's late, Billy. You go home."

Sally touched my cheek and, smiling down at me, she said, "I thank you, Billy Latham. It was a brave thing you done, comin' to fetch me."

And then she kissed me.

I was grateful for the darkness. I must have gone about seventeen shades of crimson, and my tongue got so knotted that I couldn't have said anything, even if I had known what to say. I just stood there like a fencepost, dumb, thick and insensible.

I saw Sally push open the cabin door; I heard her call Jordan's name. Then his voice came clearly to my ears. "Sally?" The door swung shut, and Tom Wansuc said, "Ye done a good night's work, Billy Latham. Now go home."

Well, I can take a hint as well as the next person, though it went against the grain to have to leave just then. I was more than a little interested to know how Sally and Jordan were getting on, but I wasn't going to argue with Tom Wansuc. I was ahead at the moment; he'd said I'd done good work, and I didn't mean to forfeit his good opinion. I reckoned that, after the jawing I'd get when I got home, I'd need all the friends I could muster.

I plodded off down the hill, tired and hot and feeling the beginnings of dread uncoiling in the pit of my stomach. But I was strangely happy, too. I'd managed to help do Jordan a good turn, and I'd had a pretty exciting time to boot. And Sally kissed me.

When I hove into my own front yard, I was distressed to see that the lamps were still burning. I guessed they burned for me. I hadn't a prayer of slipping in unnoticed, so I just took a deep breath and made my mind to take my medicine without squeaking.

Full of firm resolution, and with Sally's kiss still glowing on my cheek, I lifted the latch and let myself in.

To my astonishment, neither Father nor Mother was standing there waiting to pronounce sentence. I could hear voices coming from the kitchen, and laughter. It sounded hopeful to my guilty ears, and I began to take heart. I gave my breeches a hitch and marched myself right out to the kitchen, figuring that company does more than even a soft answer when it comes to turning away wrath.

"Halloa, Billy!" Father cried, as I entered the room. "Where've ye been?"

I blinked and looked around me. There were Colonel Ledyard, Captain Stanton, Ensign Avery, Sergeant Rufus Avery, Major Gallup, Captain Youngs Ledyard, and I disremember who else. They all seemed mighty cheerful, and I judged that the jug of Jamaica in the center of the table accounted for that. But I was only half right.

"Neighbors," said my father, getting to his feet and nearly upsetting his chair, "you all know my boy Billy."

I guess they ought to have known me. Hadn't I lugged water for 'em all that summer? But they greeted me as if I were the Prodigal Son, come home for a helping of fatted calf. Rufus Avery even raised his cup and said, "Your health, Sir!"

From the look of him, I was glad I wouldn't be wearing his head come morning.

Father put his arm around me and drew me over to stand by his chair. "Now, then, Billy, where were ye rovin' till this hour o' the night?"

That was three times he'd called me Billy, instead of Will. I guessed that he was merrier than ordinary himself, though his face didn't flame the way Rufus Avery's did. And I calculated that his good spirits were to my advantage. So I said, "Ye told me once I should stand by my friends."

Father nodded. "Gospel truth," he said. "A man has to stand by his friends. Right, Neighbors?"

His neighbors all allowed that it was so.

"Well," said I, "that's where I've been, Father, standing by a friend."

"Good lad!" cried Major Gallup. "What's a friend for, hey?"

"To friendship!" said Rufus Avery, hoisting his cup once more.

"Friendship!" echoed one and all, and another pint of rum slid down the hatch.

"What's the occasion, Father?" said I. "Have the British surrendered?"

That set 'em all to roaring, and Youngs Ledyard commenced to choke and well nigh lost his dignity — and more — when Major Gallup thumped him on the back.

"No, Sir," said Father, when he could speak. "They ain't surrendered yet. But they'd do well to quit now, before another Ledyard joins the fray."

"Another — ?"

Colonel Ledyard rose, ruddy-cheeked and smiling. "Billy," he said, "I have the honor to report the arrival in this world of a brand-new baby — my son, Charlie."

He offered his hand, so I shook it and said, "Charlie's a good name, Colonel."

"To Charlie!" cried Rufus Avery. And they all had to drink to that. Somebody, I don't recall who, suggested that I should join in the toast. Youngs Ledyard, still beet red from his near strangulation, pressed a mug on me and bid me toss it down. I looked to Father. He winked and said, "Bottom's up, boy."

I felt pretty big, I can tell ye. I raised my mug and said, "To Charlie!" And I threw my head back and let 'er slide.

Je-rusalem! I thought I'd swallowed fire! That rum hit bottom and bounced back clear to my cranium. My breathing stopped, and the water ran from my eyes in rivulets. I could almost feel the steam coming out of my ears. If I could have talked, I would have called for water, gallons of it, only my mouth wasn't working and no words would come out.

Luckily, the Colonel sensed my difficulty. He sprang to the pump and fetched me a dipperful. I drained it off and called for more. I must have put away a whole pond before the fire was finally put out.

The men enjoyed my discomfort. They laughed and whacked the table, and each other, and called out all kinds of helpful advice.

"Fight fire with fire, boy!" cried Rufus Avery, waving the jug in the air. "Have another!"

"Beware of water, Billy," thundered Captain Stanton. "It'll rust your pipes."

"Drink some buttermilk to coat your innards," Major Gallup said. "Then ye can soak up rum till the cows come home."

Well, I didn't want to appear ungrateful, but I was of no mind to sample any more of that devil's potion. "Gentlemen," said I, feeling bold and puffed up by all this notice, "I thank ye for the rum and the advice."

"Hear, hear!" cried Youngs Ledyard, banging his mug on the table.

"But," said I, "I am in the watering trade, as ye know."

" 'Tis honest work," Stanton declared, "but there's no future in it."

"That's so, Captain," said I, "but so long as I am in the trade, I think I must give it all my custom. I'll drink naught but water hereafter."

My feeble jest was greeted by more applause than it deserved, and I'm afraid my head was in a way to be turned altogether. But Father said, "Well spoke, Billy. And now to bed. We want you spry in the morning."

And so I was packed off in time to keep me from making myself a nuisance and a fool. Before I slept, I resolved to buy something handsome for little Charlie Ledyard. He'd arrived in time to save me considerable awkwardness, and I considered myself obliged.

I lugged a lot of water that next morning. There were some powerfully thirsty men about the Fort that day. I would have thought that all that drinking of the past evening would have kept 'em from thirsting for a month.

I noticed, too, that some folks were not so merry as they had been. Sergeant Avery was cross as two sticks, and Youngs Ledyard was so almighty touchy that the men took to going a half-mile out of their way to avoid attracting his eye. Father himself seemed remarkably subdued, and he didn't bustle about so brisk as usual.

One cheerful soul among us was Jordan Freeman. He fairly flung himself into his work, and whistled as he went — until Youngs Ledyard spoke up sharply and told him to for God's sake cease his noise.

That troubled Jordan not at all. He ceased whistling, but he couldn't stop grinning. And, first chance he got, he caught up with me and just lifted me clean off the ground and swung me around three times in the air.

"Wuff!" I cried. "Let me down!"

"Can't help it, Billy," he said. "I feel so good this morning, I just have to do somethin' or I'll purely bust."

"Well, don't do it to me," I said, trying to sound grumpy. "I got work to do."

"Uh-huh. You are a worker, Billy Latham, and no mistake. Seems to me you been workin' day and night. Especially night."

"What d'ye mean?"

"I mean I know ye went on a raidin' party last night, right smack into the enemy's camp."

I looked around sharp to see if anybody was listening. But the men were all busy, and the officers all suffering. There was nobody paying any mind to Jordan and me.

"Jordan," I said, "don't talk about it. My Father don't know where I was last night, and I don't mean that he should ever know."

"Ye didn't get whupped, did you, Billy?" Jordan looked so concerned that I wished I had the past night to do all over again.

"No," I said. "My luck was good all around."

"I'm glad, Billy," he said, squeezing my shoulder in his iron grasp. "I value you, boy. I don't want ye gettin' whupped on my account. Not ever."

I wanted to say many things. Most of all, I wanted to tell him that I'd take a whipping for him anytime. But I only said, "No fear, Jordan. I tell ye, my luck was good."

He nodded, "Mine, too." A beautiful smile lighted his face. "Things are goin' to be fine, Billy. I was awful low yesterday. Awful low. I felt the same as ole man Adam must've felt after bein' chased out o' the Garden. I'd forgot that I had friends. I'd forgot what good friends they are. But I know now, and I ain't ever goin' to forget again."

Now I almost wished I had been bit by that dog, or punished when I got home. I couldn't see that I deserved so much from Jordan. I felt so filled-up and proud that I just couldn't speak.

"Ye took an awful risk for me, Billy. You and Tom could have been put in jail, or shot, or both. And you did it for me." Jordan shook his head. "I marvel at it, Billy. I purely marvel."

I hadn't thought about jail or shooting. I like to think I'd have gone with Tom anyway, but I couldn't be certain. That deflated me some; and, indeed my knees commenced to knocking at the thought of the hazard I'd run.

"Well," said Jordan, "It's no good sayin' thank'ee. Sayin' don't amount to shucks. But

I owe ye, Billy. And I mean to pay you when I can."

"Friends don't pay friends," I said.

Jordan grinned wide. "We are friends, ain't we, Billy?"

"You bet," I said. "But if I don't get this water around pretty quick, you'll be about the only friend I've got in this whole blamed Fort."

We went our separate ways then, and though I was worked right down to the nub that day, my heart was light and my spirits high. Tom Wansuc turned up towards noon, having lost the whole morning drilling with the big guns on the parapet. He drew me aside and, like Jordan before him, wanted to know if I'd got skinned for coming home so late.

I told him I hadn't.

"Good." He spat in the dust and wiped his lips on the back of his hand. "Jordan seems brighter today."

"He does. Reckon mebbe Sally talked some sense into him."

"Guess so." Tom stared off towards the New London shore for a long moment, then he turned back to me and said, "He's agreed to let me lend him the money."

"Oh, Tom! That's — that's splendid!"

Tom grunted. "He said he'd wait another week or two, just to see if anything turned up. If it don't he'll borrow off me."

"Ye won't let him back out, will ye, Tom?"

A light flickered in Tom's dark eyes, and his mouth widened ever so slightly. "I'll scalp him first," he said.

"Who is goin' to approach Colonel Harris?"

"Not me." Tom almost smiled. "Jordan means to ask Colonel Ledyard to serve as go-between. He stands in good with Ledyard. Guess he'd do that for Jordan."

"I'm sure of it," I said. "The colonel's awful fond of him."

"Guess ye're right." Tom folded his massive arms across his broad bare chest. "Jordan's got good friends. He's got no money, but he's rich all the same."

"Yes," I said, picking up my bucket and making ready to head back to the well. "I hadn't thought of it that way, but he is rich, ain't he?"

I started off, but Tom said, "Wait."

"What is it?"

Tom unfolded his arms and came over to me. "I got to say this," he said, eyeing me up and down. "I don't hold much with boys gen'rally. They're a big nuisance most times. Throw stones at my house; steal truck from my garden; call me 'Big Chief,' and some other things not so good. But I like you, Billy Latham. You took a big chance last night. And you carried it off like a man."

That was the longest speech I ever heard from Tom Wansuc. I doubt he ever made a longer. And all I could think of to say was, "It was for Jordan, wasn't it? He's my friend."

"Jordan's lucky." Now Tom did smile, and he offered his hand. "Think mebbe you could be my friend, too?"

I tell ye, I felt as rich as Jordan Freeman.

CHAPTER XII

I cannot recall a time when life seemed to go better than it did in those days of August '81. Even the thought of school commencing again could not mar the sense of well-being that pervaded that golden time. All to home were well and hearty; Jordan and Tom seemed more than content; the Ledyards had their new baby to console them for the loss of Miss Sarah; and it looked to me as though the world was being governed just right. It wanted only the defeat of the British to establish perfect justice here below, and I was willing to postpone the day until I got in some licks of my own against the forces of fat King George.

I went about my work cheerfully, buoyed by the thought that soon now Jordan would contrive to buy Sally free and bring her across the Thames to keep house for him and bring their child into the world. It had been a good summer for me. I'd acquired a pair of splendid friends, had had some good times, and would end the season with money in my pocket. I guess I was about as satisfied as any boy could be.

But, though I couldn't know it, a storm was brewing, and such a blow as would sweep through my life and change it utterly. Nothing would ever be the same again.

I remember so well that last evening before the storm broke. After a long hot day at the Fort, Tom and Jordan were all for going swimming. Father said I could go along, provided I got home at a respectable hour, and off I trotted, catching up with Jordan and Tom down at the ferry. We had a fine time, just splashing about and cutting up foolish. Those two rascals chucked me in afore I could get out of my breeches, but I didn't care. There was no meanness in it. It was just their way of making fun. And I was glad to be a part of it.

We had a race, too, and though they spotted me a dozen yards, I came in last. Jordan beat. Tom said it wasn't fair, Jordan being so long and all. "You cover half the distance just by lyin' down," he said.

"Never mind," said Jordan. "When ye're all growed up, you'll have a better chance."

Tom splashed him for that. And Jordan splashed him back, and then they went at it, standing waist deep in the water and beating up a regular hurricane. It's a wonder they didn't drown each other, the way that water flew. But at last they left off and came out to sit alongside me on the bank, to smoke their pipes and watch the sun go down.

It was just lovely sitting there, listening to the lapping of the wavelets and letting the westerly breeze flow over us as the evening came on. The first star showed its pure white light; and, boylike, I made a silent wish that the three of us would always be happy as we were that night.

Jordan blew out a cloud of smoke and said, "Well, Tom, reckon I'll talk to the Colonel tomorrow."

" 'Bout Sally?"

Jordan nodded. "Been shilly-shallyin' long enough, I guess. If I'm bound to put my neck in the noose, there's no point in delayin' longer."

"Nice way to talk," Tom muttered. "You told Sally?"

"Last night." Jordan grinned. "She was mighty pleased about it."

Tom shook his head. "Can't figger it," he said. "Smart gal like that."

Lazy as a big old cat, Jordan just stretched out his arm and gave Tom a shove. There was a yell, a splash, and next thing I knew there was an Injun in the river. Tom came up spouting water and some strong language. Jordan, chuckling, got up on his knees and leaned over to lend Tom a hand. That was his mistake. Tom grasped his hand and, with a sharp tug, he pulled Jordan in on top of him.

Those two great babies thrashed around in the shallows like a pair of fighting sharks, churning up the water and cussing and laughing and promising to do all kinds of dreadful things to each other. How it might have ended I couldn't say. Neither one was of a mind to let up, and both was about half-drowned. But suddenly Jordan let out a yelp. "Jellyfish!" he cried, leaping half out of the water.

"Ouch! Dammit! They got me, too," roared Tom. And the two of them came out of the drink pretty lively.

If ye've ever been stung by a jellyfish, you know it smarts. Your skin feels like there's about a thousand needles jabbing into you, and ye can't do anything but hop around till the sting wears off. I had to cackle to see those two capering up and down the bank. It wanted only a fiddle to turn the show into a dance.

"He thinks it's funny," growled Tom Wansuc, pointing at me.

"Let's give him a taste of it," Jordan said, laying hold of me.

"Give them jellyfish a taste of him, ye mean," said Tom, grabbing an arm.

"No, no!" I hollered. "Jordan, Tom, don't!"

Jordan glanced over at Tom. "What d'ye say, Tom?"

"We-ll, no sense in wastin' bait," he said. "Save it for when we go fishin."

"Ye got off this time," Jordan told me. "But don't you crowd your luck now, or I might have to change my mind."

I told him I'd behave, and he let go his hold. He and Tom smoked another pipe, and Jordan talked on about how fine things would be once he and Sally settled down.

"We'll have us a garden," he said, "and some chickens, and a cow. Got to have a cow. Babies require whole oceans of milk, ye know."

Tom Wansuc snorted. "Great snakes, Jordan! Ye're turnin' into a reg'lar ol' woman. Reckon I won't have nobody to hunt or fish with now."

"I'll go with ye, Tom," I said.

I felt the weight of Tom's hand on my knee. "Thank'ee Billy Latham," he said. "Reckon I have got a partner after all."

"Shucks, Tom. Reckon I'll still be your partner even if I am married," Jordan said.

Tom shook his head. "Nossir," he said, "it don't ever work that way. A man gets married, and he can't call his time his own. That Sally'll make you toe the line, Jordan. She'll call the tune, and you'll dance to it."

"Pooh!"

"So ye say. D'you reckon Sally will want

me comin' around to call? You reckon she'll let me track dirt on her floors, and smoke up the house, and sit up with ye till all hours? I guess not."

"Huh! I guess she better not try to stop ye. I'm head of that house, I reckon, and free to do as I please."

"Free! Why, Jordan, you was freer when Colonel had the papers on ye than any husband ever was or will be."

I was blessed if I knew who was in the right of it. I had to allow the power of Tom's argument, but I just couldn't believe that Sally would be the kind to try to keep Jordan on a short leash. I made up my mind to watch and see how matters went. If a man like Jordan could be tamed and stabled by a slip of a gal like Sally, then I'd know marrying was not for me. I doubted she could do it, but I meant to bide my time and see.

The debate died away unresolved, with Jordan saying that Tom would find out, and Tom saying he guessed he would.

It was getting dark, and Jordan said, "We'd better steer for home, Tom. We don't want Billy to catch it from his pa."

I was of no mind to go, but I told myself that there was always tomorrow. We got our clothes on and headed up the bank. What a lovely night it was! The air was heavy with honeysuckle, and seasoned with salt; the breeze was cool; the sky studded over with stars. It was so still ye could have heard a fly light on a frog's back two miles off. At our backs the river seemed asleep, and before us the village lay, peaceful and at rest.

We sauntered along to my father's house, and I bid Tom and Jordan good night and turned in at the gate. As I hove around to the back yard, I spied Father sitting on the back step, puffing away on his old clay pipe.

" 'Evenin', Will," he said.

" 'Evenin', Father."

"Light a spell," he said, moving over and making room for me. "Have a good swim, did ye?"

"Splendid," I said. "The water's warm as anything."

Father tapped the dottle of his pipe into his palm. "Seems like any amount o' years since you and I went swimmin', Will. Always did like takin' you along on outin's — fishin' or huckleberryin' or nuttin' in the fall. We had good times then."

"We did."

Father stowed his pipe in his pocket. "I don't know why 'tis, Will, but seems like fathers and sons don't get so many years together. A boy grows up almost without ye noticin', and all the while ye get busier and busier, and next thing ye know, whole years have slipped by, and all of a sudden ye realize ye've missed out on so many good times."

"But we did have some all the same," I said.

"It's this cussed war," Father went on, almost as if he hadn't heard me. "It takes up so much of my time that I don't even notice the seasons turnin'. Summer and winter and spring all run together so, and another year's gone afore I've got used to bein' a year older."

He sighed and shook his head. "I meant to spend more time with ye, boy. I truly meant to. I'd hoped to learn ye how to shoot, and how to stick to a hoss and sail a boat and such like. Looks like I've missed out on all of it."

"No ye haven't, Father," I said, trying to cheer him. "There's lots of years yet before I'm all grown."

"Not so many, Will," he said, roughing my hair. "Not so many."

Then he heaved a sigh and got to his feet. "Well, we'll just have to try and make the most of what time we got left, hey?"

"We will, Father."

"Certain, we will. War or no war, I mean to go deer huntin' soon as the weather cools down. Reckon you'd like to come along?"

"I guess," I said, with considerable gusto.

"Good, then. We'll fit ye out with some kind of musket, and we'll put in some time learnin' ye to load and shoot. I guess us Lathams'll be more'n a match for any fat buck roamin' these parts, hey?"

"You bet!"

Father laughed. "Well," he said, "ye better get along in now, Will. Got another day's work ahead of us come mornin'."

"Good night, Father," I said.

" 'Night, Will."

I went into the house and on up to my garret chamber. But I couldn't bear to turn in just yet. I sat by my window and gazed out over the slumbering town. I felt strangely mournful, yet happy at the same time. Another summer was nearly gone, and that was enough to make anybody feel kind of solemn and sad. Yet it had been a splendid time, a time to look back on and be glad of always.

My mind turned on the words Father had said about time passing and whole years slipping by. That made me so melancholy, I came near to weeping. Time, it seemed to me, was a lot like my river. It just kept flowing on forever, and no man could stop it or turn it aside. It just rolled on, never ceasing, till it emptied out into — what?

The days and weeks and months were like so many drops of water, tumbling downstream, all blending together so ye couldn't distinguish one from another. The river was new every day, yet it looked always the same, only its color changing to reflect the changing sky. So too with time. It flows on over the people around you, and ye don't notice any change from day to day. But then, at some point, one by one, people let go their hold and go a-drifting down the stream, never to return.

I couldn't bear to think about it anymore. I got up, went over to my bed, knelt down and said my prayers. That comforted me some, and I hopped into bed and was soon fast asleep.

Next thing I knew, there was a thunderous banging at my door, and I heard Father calling, "Look alive, Will! Ye're needed down below!"

I sprang out of bed and hustled into my clothes, not troubling to wash up. There was insistence in Father's tone that would not admit of delay. I skinned down the stairs at a lively clip and headed for the kitchen on the run.

"There ye are, Will," said Father. "Sit down and load in some porridge. Likely ye'll need it afore this day is through."

For all that it was so awful early and I was so drugged with sleep, I noticed right off that Father had on his old Army coat, and slung over his shoulder was the powder horn he'd carried at Dorchester Heights. When I was younger, I used to love to play with that horn. Father had carved on it a picture of Boston Harbor, ships and all, with his jackknife, and it was my special pleasure to just stare at that carving and try to imagine Father up there in Massachusetts, carving that picture while he waited for the battle to begin.

"What's amiss, Father?" I said.

"It's come, Will," he replied, reaching down his musket from its place of honor over the hearth. "Rufus Avery was just here. Thirty-two sail have been spotted off Eastern Point. Looks like the Reg'lars mean to pay us off for takin' the *Hannah*."

My porridge stuck in my throat. Father was talking just as calm as if he were getting ready to go horse-trading, or maybe take a load of grain to the mill. But my head was spinning like a top. I heard every word he was saying, but it was as if he was talking from far off. His words came at me through a kind of fog, and I was having a deal of trouble just sorting 'em out and stringing 'em together in a way that made sense.

"Your mother and the gals are gatherin' up their val'ables, and I've told off Lambo to drive 'em over to your Uncle Avery's in Poquonnock Plain. I don't know that the

Reg'lars mean to raid the village, but I can't take that chance.

"Ye're to go with the family, Will. I look to you to play a man's part today. Understand?"

I swallowed hard, and that gob of porridge went down like a plummet to the bottom of my stomach. It lay there like lead.

"D'ye understand me, Will?"

"Y-yessir," I said.

"They say that bastard Arnold is in command o' the force," he said. "God grant he sets foot on Groton Bank, boy, and I get one clean shot at him. He'll howl in Hell tonight, if I do."

Just then Mother came in from the parlor we so seldom used, Luke in her arms, and Mary, Eunice and Lucy at her heels. The gals were loaded down with bundles and sacks crammed with everything from candlesticks to hard money. Mother, head high, her cheeks mantled pink, her eyes shining, looked at me and said, "Will, give your sisters a hand with these articles. Pile 'em by the back step, then go and stir up Lambo and tell him to bring the wagon 'round."

"Yes, Ma'am," I said. I took my share of the things and ploughed through the back door and out into the dawning light. I set my burden down and, leaving the gals to struggle with theirs, I lit out for the barn.

"Lambo!" I shouted. "Hey, Lambo! Hitch up, darn ye, and bring that wagon 'round!"

"I'm hurryin', Mast' Billy. Movin' just as fast's I can."

I guess he was, too. For by the time I reached our barn, out came the wagon with our good old sorrel gelding, Major, and Jenny, the white mare, in the traces.

"Here I am, Mast' Billy," Lambo said.

"I can see that, blame it. I've got eyes." I jumped up onto the seat beside him. "Drive 'round to the back door, and we'll load on all the plunder."

We rumbled across the yard to where the gals were standing, and in just about two shakes, Lambo and I piled that stuff into the wagon. Then he and I handed the gals on up, and they got themselves situated as best they could amid the heaped up bundles.

Father and Mother appeared in the doorway just as Lucy settled herself down on the best featherbed. I never saw Father stand so straight and proud. He looked mighty handsome, I can tell ye; and Mother was just blooming. She clung to his arm and looked up at him, her great eyes glowing with love and pride.

"All loaded, Will?" said Father.

"Yes, Sir."

"Except for this precious packet," said Mother, laughing as she handed Luke on up to my sister Mary.

"Now I guess we are ready, Father," I said.

"Good boy." He turned to Mother and kissed her full on the mouth.

"Eunice," he said, "I reckon ye'll be safe over to Avery's. I'll come for ye when I can."

Mother, her eyes glistening, smiled up at him. "You look out for yourself, Will Latham. Don't worry about us."

Father nodded, and I was startled to see that his own eyes were brimming. He sniffed loudly, and passed his hand over his mouth. Then he said, "Well, God bless ye, old gal. I — I reckon I better be goin'."

He turned to me. "You help your mother up, Will. And you, Lambo —"

"Yessir, Mast' Will?"

"You drive fast, but careful, hear? Get the family safe through, then you ask Elder Avery for the loan of his musket, and get yourself back to the Fort. We'll need every able-bodied man we can muster."

"Yessir, Mast' Will. I'll do 'er."

"Move out, then! And God keep you all."

"Father —"

"What is it, Will?"

"Father, be careful."

Father smiled. He reached out his hand and tapped me lightly on the cheek. "I will, boy," he said. Then he turned and strode off rapidly in the direction of Fort Griswold.

"Come, Will," said Mother, her voice firm and controlled. "Hand me up, now. We mustn't waste another minute."

I handed her up to Lambo, then climbed up myself and perched beside her on the seat. Lambo unlimbered his switch and hollered, "Go 'long, Jenny! Gee-up, thar, Major!"

As we cleared the yard, I could not help looking back to see my father growing smaller and smaller as we pulled away.

"Don't, Will," my mother said. "Don't look back. It ain't lucky."

Lambo kept the horses moving. He took the rough road through Dark Hollow Woods, and we were all jouncing along like so many popcorn kernels in a hot skillet. But nobody murmured and nobody peeped. We were each too occupied with his own thoughts and his own fears to do much besides just hang on and worry.

There were any number of folks moving out of the village, on horse, in carts and on foot. But, though we passed many that we knew, there was no greeting and no neighboring along the way. It was if we were all fleeing Sodom as the brimstone rained down, and every soul was saving his wind for a long hard run.

Yet, even as we clipped along under the arching branches of the trees on either side, I kept hearing over and over inside my head, "Wrong way, wrong way, wrong way."

The Fort, my Fort, where I had labored all that summer, was receding farther and farther to the west. And the men, Jordan, Tom, the whole tribe of Averys, Ledyards, Stanton, and Father — oh, Father! — all were staying behind to face God knows what danger. And here was I, flying away through the woods with the womenfolk and the baby, to hide out till the danger had passed.

I look to you to play a man's part today.

My father's words came back to me as clearly as if he were seated beside me on the retreating wagon. A man's part! Hot tears of anger flooded my eyes, and I could feel a burning in my breast. Was this a man's part? To run away when danger threatened my village, my Fort, my neighbors?

I gritted my teeth so hard it made my jaws ache. I was scared and shamed and mad clear through.

Then I heard it. From far off there came a muffled roar. Then another.

"The alarm gun," Lambo said.

But, to my surprise, there followed yet a

third reverberating boom.

"That's three, Lambo," I said. "The 'larum's s'posed to be two."

"Three means a prize ship's taken, Mast' Billy."

"Don't I know that?" I hadn't meant to sound so cross, but I was at war inside myself, and I couldn't have been civil to save my soul. I was puzzled, too. Why had three cannon spoke? It made no sense at all. I gave it up, and just held on for the duration of the ride.

By the time Lambo drove the horses up into Elder Parke Avery's yard, I was calm and cold. The fever in my brain had died down, and the fire in my breast had turned to ice. My mind was made up. Father had said I must play a man's part. Very well. I would. And I resolved to play it as became my father's son.

My uncle came hobbling out of the house, my aunt right behind him, as our wagon halted before his door.

"Well, Eunice," he said, helping Mother down, "our day of tribulation's come, hey?"

"Mebbe so, Parke," Mother said. "Mebbe so. It's in God's hands now, His and William Ledyard's."

My uncle helped Lambo and me unload, while my aunt, making a great fuss over the baby, led Mother and the gals into the house, all of 'em clucking away like a flock of chickens.

"There," said my uncle, as Lambo and I set down the last bundle, "that's that."

"Mast' Parke," said Lambo, "Mast' Will said I was to ax ye for the loan of a musket so's I can go back to the Fort and help kill the English."

"Gladly, Lambert, gladly," the old gentleman said. "I only wish I was spry enough to go along with ye. Come along in. I think I have just the thing for ye."

I hung back till Lambo and my uncle disappeared into the house; then, quick as a cat, I nipped up into the wagon, slid under the tarpaulin, and lay low, not moving, not breathing, scarce daring even to think.

It was stifling under that covering, and the boards of the wagon were wonderfully hard and splintery. I suppose I hadn't been under there more than five minutes before I heard the door slam and the voices of Lambo and my uncle as they approached the wagon, but it seemed like five years. As they drew near, I fairly hugged the boards, pressing my whole body right into the wood.

"Well, Lambert," I heard my uncle say, "stand by Captain Latham."

"I mean to, Mast' Parke, live or die."

"May the Lord protect ye. And the captain, too."

"Amen," said Lambo, and I heard him climb up onto the seat. "I'll put my trust in Jesus, Mast' Parke, and in this good ol' musket."

He whipped up the horses then, and away we flew, back through Dark Hollow Woods to where there was man's work waiting to be done.

CHAPTER XIII

It was a rough passage. Lambo didn't spare the horses any, and I got thoroughly shaken up as we went careening along back through the woods to Groton. I was raising a fine crop of bruises, and every jolt seemed to go right through me, but I kept mum and stayed under cover. It didn't suit my purpose to be found out just yet.

As I bounced along, cooking to a turn under that cover, I heard again that strange three-gun signal. It was purely a mystery to me, and I could only conclude that either the signal had been changed without my knowing it or, what was less likely, that a prize had actually been taken. I doubted the former, and altogether discounted the latter. Rufus Avery was no fool. He would not have roused my father at four in the morning unless he had really seen the enemy approaching. Well, I reckoned that if I survived the ride, I'd have some answers shortly.

When I judged we were well clear of Poquonnock Plain, I raised the corner of the tarpaulin a mite to let in some air. But it wasn't till I felt the wagon halt and heard familiar voices calling out to Lambo that I crawled out from under — and found myself face-to-face with Father.

I was flat on my belly, and he was standing at the rear of the wagon with Colonel Ledyard, Captain Stanton, and old Benadam Gallup, who had served as a colonel in the French War.

It would be hard to say who was the more startled, Father or me. His jaw dropped about a foot, and his eyebrows shot up almost to the rim of his tricorn hat. As for me, well, I just lay there staring up at him, popeyed and gaping, unable to utter a single word.

Colonel Ledyard, looking mighty smart in his coat with the gold epaulettes and the gleaming buttons, was first to speak. "Billy," he said, "what on earth are ye doing here?"

"I-I come to help," I said.

"Lambo!" cried Father, finding his voice at last, "Did you have any part in this?"

"N-nossir, Mast' Will, indeed I did not." Poor Lambo. He could not have been more plainly innocent had an archangel come down from Heaven and stood alongside him.

"It wasn't Lambo's doin', Father," said I, getting up on my hind legs. "I ducked in under the tarpaulin when he wasn't lookin'."

Father frowned and looked terribly stern. "I sent ye to your uncle's to look after your mother, boy," he said.

"I did that, Father. She and Luke and the gals are all snug and safe."

"I meant for you to be safe, too."

"I had to come, Father. Ye said you wanted me to play a man's part today. I couldn't do that hiding out over to Uncle Avery's."

"If ye like, Captain Latham, I'll detail a man to escort the boy out of harm's way," Ledyard said.

Father ran his tongue over his teeth for a bit, then he sniffed and said, "Guess not, Colonel. We can't spare a soul. The boy's here; reckon he'll have to stay. He'll do to pass powder and shot I guess."

I was jubilant, but I had sense enough not to crow any. I'd pushed my luck about as far as it could go, and the only sane course for me now was to keep mum, look sharp and make myself useful.

"You stay by me for now, Will," Father said, his tone softer now, and something close to a smile crossing his face. "I'll assign ye to your post directly."

I skipped down from the wagon and went over to stand by Father. Plainly, I'd come at a critical time. Ledyard and his officers had been holding a council, and I had come rolling in right in the middle of it. Now they resumed their pow-wow, and I was a most interested listener, I can promise ye.

"You were saying, Captain Stanton," said Ledyard, "that ye favor abandoning the Fort."

Stanton scratched the stubble on his cheek, snorted, and said, "Well, I wouldn't put it jest the way, Colonel. But, judging from the number o' sail standin' off the Point, I calc'late there must be well nigh two thousand o' them as against less'n two hunnert of us. Even if they was to split up and send half their troops against New London, we'd still have a thousand Reg'lars comin' at us.

"They've gone and sp'iled the 'larum by firin' that third gun, so I guess we needn't look for no more of your men to turn up."

So that was it! The enemy, whether they knew our signal or only guessed at it, had rendered it ineffective by firing off a cannon of their own.

Stanton went on. "I think it would be prudent to mebbe fire off a salvo to slow 'em up a little, then spike our guns and light out. We can skirmish with 'em as they come on, the way we done at Lexington. Those fools will just keep to their silly formation, the way they allus do. And we can disperse, take cover, and just bang away at 'em from behind trees and fences and such. We'll do a lot more damage that way, and mebbe save our skins in the bargain.

"If they was to ketch us inside this here Fort of yours," Stanton shook his grizzled head, "well, Colonel, there'd be any number o' widders and orphans in this town by nightfall."

"Ye think the Fort's less than secure, then, Captain?"

"Secure? 'Course it's secure, and strong, too, and well made. But, Colonel, without a force to hold it, ye'd do better to leave it while you can and light out for the woods!"

"Hem!" Old Benadam Gallup spoke up. "I have to differ with ye, Neighbor Stanton."

"Do ye?"

The old warrior rocked back and forth on the balls of his feet. "Yes, Sir, I do. In the fust place, this Fort's solid as any in New England. Second, if we was to leave it and scatter, what's to keep the Reg'lars from lootin' and burnin' and raisin' Hell in general? Our helter-skelter sharpshootin' won't slow 'em down much, only harrass 'em and make 'em mad.

"And, finally, as to your point about numbers, I judge that I could ride out even now and, inside of an hour or two, muster anywhere from three to six hundred men from around the countryside." Old Benadam swelled up like a bullfrog, looking mighty satisfied at having played his trump card.

"Could ye do that, Colonel?" asked Ledyard, pleasing the old fellow by giving him his title.

"Certain, Sir. Just say the word, and I'll ride out at once."

"What say the rest of ye?" Ledyard inquired. "Cap'n Latham?"

Father rubbed his jaw thoughtfully, then he said, "If Colonel Gallup can bring in another two or three hunnert, even, I guess we could stand 'em off all right. I admit, Colonel, I'd be mighty sorry to spike our guns. They speak with considerable authority. 'Sides, some of the men have no muskets. If we was to quit the Fort, we'd have even less workin' for us than we do now."

Ledyard nodded. Then he polled his other captains — 'Lijah and 'Lisha Avery, Samuel and Simeon Allyn, Hubbard Burrows, Solomon Perkins, Nathan Moore, John Williams and Youngs Ledyard. All were for staying. Youngs Ledyard, his eyes fever bright, declared that Fort Griswold was "impregnable and invincible."

He judged we were safer there than we'd be anywhere else, and stronger, too.

The Colonel smiled. "I pray we are,

Nephew," he said. "Well, then, we stay."

"Fair enough," said Stanton. "You may rely on me to do my part."

"I am certain of that, Sir," Ledyard said. Then he turned to Benadam Gallup. "You will oblige us, Sir, if you will ride out now and muster all ye can. Your brother, the Major, is by this time at Lebanon, reporting our situation to Governor Trumbull. I have no doubt that we can look for relief from that quarter in good season. Major Gallup was with me in New London earlier this morning, and rode out afore sunrise."

"I'll go at once," Benadam Gallup said. He hoisted himself up astride his horse and went out the gate at a canter, with Ledyard's hearty "Godspeed!" ringing in his ears.

It was about nine o'clock. With luck, we could look for reinforcements before noon. If Arnold would oblige us by waiting till then before making his move, we stood a fair chance of thwarting his purpose. But Arnold was of no mind to wait. Scarcely had Benadam Gallup quit the Fort when a cry went up from the sentry on the parapet. "They're movin' on Fort Trumbull!"

There came the thunder of cannon, then a sudden, awful stillness followed by human voices crying out in anger and pain. Ledyard and his officers dashed to the rampart, and

I ran right along after 'em. We scaled the ladders in about two shakes and took up positions overlooking the river.

To the southwest, we could see boatloads of Reg'lars and green-jacketed Hessians pulling for the beach below the New London light under a cloud of smoke. There must have been fully seven hundred of 'em. And Adam Shapley, captain of Fort Trumbull, had but two dozen men in his command.

"Adam, Adam," muttered Ledyard, "spike your guns and fly."

I saw a puff of smoke from Fort Trumbull, then heard a shuddering whump! One after another, the guns of Trumbull spoke, heaving grape and ball at the anchored fleet. We sent up a cheer as the shot tore through the rigging of the enemy's ships, but there was no real damage inflicted that I could see.

"Shapley's leaving!" Youngs Ledyard cried. "Look there!"

Tiny figures of men came running down to the sand. We watched, helpless, as they struggled to push off their boats.

"They're a-comin' this way!"

But his joy and ours was short-lived, for the rattle of musketry came to our ears, and we could see the balls kicking up water all around the Fort Trumbull boats. They were being fired on from the fleet, and at such close range that many a ball found its mark in human flesh.

"Lord A'mighty!" cried Father. "Row, dammit! Pull for your lives!"

I doubted any such advice was needed. We could see the men straining at their oars, but though they made the water fly, it seemed an eternity before they were out of range.

"Sergeant Chester!" Ledyard roared.

"Here, Colonel!" Eldridge Chester came on the run.

"Sergeant, take a party of men and run down to receive Captain Shapley and his men. Bring 'em into the Fort."

"Yes, sir."

"Would to God the Downers were here to treat the wounded," Ledyard growled.

The Downers, father and son, were respectively surgeon and assistant-surgeon of the 8th Regiment, Connecticut Militia. Indeed, Avery, the son, had seen duty as rank-and-file before he'd been named to assist his father. They resided in Preston, near Norwich, some fourteen miles upriver. We learned later that they, too, had been confused by the "sp'iled alarum," as Captain Stanton had put it, and so, like many of our neighbors, had not come to the Fort.

Sergeant Chester told off a dozen men, and they went charging off down the slope to the waterfront. And even as we watched, the enemy troops landed in New London. We could see their bright coats sharp and clear from more than a mile off, as they scurried like green and scarlet bugs up the white sandy beach.

"Je-rusalem!" Father said. "There's a number of 'em."

"Colonel Ledyard!"

Ledyard turned and saw Lieutenant William Starr mounting the parapet. "What is it?" he said.

"Sir, Andy Billings just came sliding in through the gate as we were locking up. He says the Reg'lars have landed at Eastern Point."

"Send him to me, Mr. Starr. At once."

"Here I am, Colonel," cried a youthful voice, and Andy Billings's head appeared above the platform. He clambered up and came to attention before his commander.

"Corporal Billings, make your report."

"Yes, Sir. Well," Andy's chest was heaving, and he was fighting to get his breath. "I was hoein' out in the cornfield, ye see, and I heard the guns go off, but didn't think much of it, there bein' three of 'em, and that meanin' only —"

"Yes, yes. Get to the point, man. Ye say the enemy has landed?"

"Yes, Sir. I had a mind to go down to the Point to cool off a bit, and then I see all them ships. Land o' Goshen, Colonel! The whole blamed British navy must be here today. I never see —"

"Corporal, to the point, if ye please."

"Yes, Sir. Well. When I seen them ships, I kind of hunched down behind a fence to watch what would happen. And, great God A'mighty, about a thousand of 'em put out in boats and commenced to rowin' straight towards me."

"A thousand, ye say?"

"Must be damned near that, Colonel, with carriages and guns, too, and some hosses to draw the guns with."

"Was Arnold with them?"

"He might a-been, and he might not. I didn't stay around to look for him."

Ledyard smiled. "No, no. I guess ye wouldn't."

"No, Sir. I lit right out for the Fort, and damned if they wa'n't about to shut the gate on me. Good thing I come when I did."

Ledyard nodded. "Yes, it is, Corporal Billings, I am heartily glad that —"

"Fire!" my father shouted. "Look! Those scum are firing the houses!"

It was true. From our vantage point, we could see the shops and houses strung out along the beach, circling Mill Cove, and marching up Town Hill. Evidently, the invaders meant to destroy the stores and shipping along the wharf, but whether or not their incendiary purpose went beyond that, the fact is that the leaping flames, fanned by the southeasterly wind, quickly spread to private dwellings and public buildings. The whole western horizon was a pall of black smoke, and bright orange flames leaped high along the waterfront.

"God damn them!" cried Youngs Ledyard, his handsome face gone deathly pale. "God damn them all to Hell!"

"Je-sus, will ye look at it," muttered Stanton, slack-jawed and wide-eyed in horror and dismay. "Them poor people!"

"It's Arnold's way," said Ledyard, his voice controlled and low. "He always did favor fire as a tool of war, and ye can believe me when I tell you that he means to level the town. Look! Look there! The courthouse! Aye, and the church, too!"

Through the haze we could make out the buildings he cited. They stood on a high rise at the top of the Parade, and our view was unobstructed save for the mantle of smoke hanging over the town. Flames were licking up the sides of the church and dancing over the roof of the courthouse. And if I escape

Hell at the end, I am not likely to see such a scene again.

"The whole town's going up," muttered Father. "And that for the taking of the *Hannah*!"

With the wind steady from the southeast, the smoke was blown away from us as it rose, and we could distinguish throngs of folk fleeing in panic towards Quaker Hill to the north. We could make out, too, uniformed men running through the streets with torches in their hands. There could be no doubt now that they were bent on savagery. British or Hessian, it made no difference. These were Arnold's troops, soldiers of the Crown, and they were conducting themselves like a Mohawk war party, mad with the lust for blood and vengeance.

"Yonder comes Chester with Captain Shapley, Colonel," remarked Captain Perkins. "There's wounded among 'em."

Up the slope the Trumbull garrison came, nearly one third of them being carried or helped up the steep incline. Once inside the Fort, Shapley lost no time in reporting to Ledyard.

It was a moving sight, I can tell ye, to see those two strong men embrace. Shapley, the tears streaming down his face, said, "Sir, I am sorry to have left my post."

"You did right, Captain. We need you here," Ledyard replied. "Ye're worth far more to us alive in Groton than dead in New London."

Shapley turned and looked out across the Thames at the stricken town. "If God sees this, and I am sure He does, He will not let those butchers go unpunished."

"We mean to punish 'em some, Cap'n," Amos Stanton declared. "With your Fort Trumbull boys to help us, I reckon we'll dose a few with some lead pills afore the day's over."

"We couldn't ask for better artillerymen than these," Ledyard said. "Now, if our reinforcements would only arrive —"

"Colonel!" A sentry sang out from the southwest bastion. "Enemy's approaching!"

"To your posts!" Ledyard cried. "Captains, come with me!"

Well, as I had no post as yet, I took up the rear and trotted along after Father and the other officers. We drew up alongside the sentry and looked down to where a party of redcoats was emerging from the woods under a white flag.

They looked almighty soldierly in their brilliant uniforms, their white belts standing out sharply against the scarlet of their coats. On they came, marching, marching, steady, relentless, seemingly unafraid.

"You may fire a warning, Sentry," Ledyard said.

The sentry, a great farm boy by the name of Wait Lester, got off a shot that kicked up dust about a yard in front of the first rank. The enemy officer called a halt, about forty rods off from where we stood.

"Captain Shapley," said Ledyard, "I'd be obliged if you and Captains Avery, Stanton and Williams would carry a flag to the enemy and parley with them."

"Yes, Sir," Shapley said. They made up a flag of Wait Lester's shirt, tied it to a pike, and marched out to treat with the Reg'lars.

Our men, even with a giant like Amos Stanton among 'em, looked small somehow, and hardly a match for the Britishers that waited to receive 'em. My heart dropped down around my ankles as I watched 'em go. I would not have stood in Adam Shapley's shoes for all the tea at the bottom of Boston Harbor.

They weren't long about it. We couldn't hear what was said, of course, but we saw Shapley salute in proper military fashion, and we could tell that some words were exchanged. In a minute or so, Shapley saluted again, wheeled about, and led his party back to the safety of the Fort.

"They are two divisions, Sir," Shapley told

Ledyard, "including a contingent of Hessians and a corps of New Jersey tories, led by a Colonel Eyre and a Major Montgomery. They demand surrender."

Ledyard's reply was drowned out in a roar from Fort Trumbull, we turned in time to see a middling big splash as the ball fell short and drowned itself in the river.

"They must have got one of my guns working again," said Shapley, mildly. "I must say, I resent being banged away at with my own powder."

Ledyard turned to Wait Lester. "Sentry," he said, "relay the order to open fire on Fort Trumbull. 'Twill keep our men amused while this parleying goes on. We can shoot down into Trumbull quite handily, I judge, but their shot cannot touch us up here on the Heights."

Wait passed the order along in a bellow loud enough to shatter glass, and it was a treat to see our men spring to life as if glad of something to do. I caught a glimpse of Jordan, running up to load one of the eighteen-pounders, and I longed to sing out, so glad was I to see him. But it seemed unsoldierly to do so, so I held my peace.

"Now, my friends," said Ledyard, "do we accommodate this Colonel Eyre and surrender?"

"No, by Heavens," Youngs Ledyard cried.

"No surrender. Never, never!"

"Your response is what I expected, Captain," murmured the Colonel. "How say ye all?"

"Fight!" was the general reply.

Just then, our guns let fly at Fort Trumbull, and it was a heartening sound to hear.

"Damn!" said Shapley. "I hope they don't break open my cask of madeira."

"A pity ye didn't bring it with ye, Adam," Stanton said. "We've dry work ahead of us, or I'm a Hessian."

"Captain Shapley," said Ledyard, "you and your party may return with your flag. My compliments to Colonel Eyre. We will not surrender."

"Very good, Sir," said Shapley. And he and the others sallied forth once more. They were back even sooner this time, and all the while, the leisurely duel between ourselves and the enemy occupying Fort Trumbull continued.

"Well, Captain?" Ledyard clasped his hands behind his back and fixed Shapley with a quizzical eye.

"They are relaying your message to their commander, Colonel."

"Very well. Now, men, our reinforcements have yet to arrive. They must come, surely. And it is up to us to hold this Fort until they do. I know that I can rely on each one of ye to do his duty. I ask no more than that.

"It is regrettable that Arnold did not come up river and dispatch Eyre and his troops up the western slope. There is where we are strongest, and I have no doubt that we could, in that case, hold 'em off indefinitely. But," he shook his head, and his face went somber despite his light, almost cheerful manner of speaking, "coming at us from this direction, the Reg'lars cheat us of the use of our main battery. We shall have hard work holding 'em off till help arrives."

"There's their flag again, Sir," Shapley remarked. "I expect they'll have something to say to us."

"And I expect we all can guess what that is. Well, go to 'em, Captain. Let us hear their worst."

The little band of captains was gone a good while this time, and when they returned, their faces were set hard, their eyes dark and glowering.

"They say if they take the Fort by storm, they'll put martial law in force, Colonel," Shapley said. "It means the sword and bayonet for any that are left alive."

"Ye may tell 'em, Captain Shapley, that we will not give up the Fort, let the consequences be what they may." Ledyard spoke calmly, quietly, but there was grandeur in his bearing and a glory in his eyes.

It was an awful solemn moment. We all sensed it. And I, for my part, felt a cold chill creeping up my spine. But 'Lijah Avery rescued us all from the tyranny of our thoughts. "By God, Colonel," he said, "I hope that's an end to it. I'm gettin' mighty tired o' walkin' back and forth with that damned flag."

The men laughed, Ledyard with them. "I share your weariness, Captain," he said. "Take them my message, and repair at once to this spot."

"Captain Latham?"

"Sir?"

"Muster the men. I mean to speak to 'em before the action begins."

The flag went forth, and Father went off to summon the men. By the time Shapley and his flag had returned, the whole garrison, about one hundred and fifty strong, were gathered on the parade. I saw Jordan, looming head and shoulders above the rest, with Tom Wansuc right beside him. I reckoned my place was in the ranks, too, so I trotted on down and squeezed in between Jordan and Tom.

"Lord God A'mighty, Billy!" Jordan cried. "What are you doin' here?"

"Same thing you are, I guess."

Tom Wansuc shook his head. "I feel mighty sorry for them English now that Billy Latham's here." He squeezed my arm and said, "I sure didn't expect to see you today, Wildcat."

Jordan didn't appear to share Tom's pleasure. "Billy," he said, "why in time did ye come? You could —"

"Silence in the ranks!" Rufus Avery's voice rang out. We hushed up then, and stood easy, waiting to hear what the Colonel had to say. He didn't waste any words.

"Men," he said, "we can expect to engage the enemy shortly. As yet, the reinforcements we are expecting have not showed. It is up to us to resist the attack with all our strength, and to hold out till our comrades come. I am proud to be leading you this day. I charge you all to so conduct yourselves that you may yourselves be forever proud of what ye do here.

"As for myself, if I must lose honor or life today, you who know me best can tell which it will be.

"Our cause is just. We cannot ask a better. May God Almighty strengthen you to your task; may He protect and bless you all.

"Stand to your guns!"

At that, the men broke and ran for their posts. But Jordan knelt and seized me by the arms. "Billy, Billy," he said, "ye should not have come."

" 'Course he should have, Jordan," said Tom. "He's our reinforcements."

Troubled as he was, Jordan had to smile. "What are we goin' to do with this scamp, Tom?"

Tom grunted. "Mebbe we could stuff him in a cannon and shoot him at redcoats."

"Reckon he'd cut a pretty wide swath at that." Then the smile faded from Jordan's face. "All the same, Billy, I wish ye hadn't come."

"I had to," I said, grinning up at him. "I feared ye might get thirsty at your work."

CHAPTER XIV

It was, I judge, about eleven o'clock when the Reg'lars made their move. I'd been told off to hustle powder and shot, so I could catch only glimpses of the goings-on as I hipered to and from the several cannon.

The honor of drawing first blood fell to Captain Elias Halsey, a privateersman from Long Island who had turned up with Shapley's men from Fort Trumbull. Ledyard, knowing Halsey to be an expert gunner, had assigned him to one of the big thumpers in the southwest bastion. The British had divided their forces, and while Major Montgomery was leading his men around to the east of us, Colonel Eyre and his troops were coming up from the southwest. As Eyre's division came within range, Halsey greeted them with a charge of grape. A score of redcoats went down before the blast; their comrades scattered, re-formed, and came on at the quick march, trailing their arms.

Father's men, meanwhile, were heaving shot into Montgomery's ranks with good effect. Jordan and Tom were serving in his battery, and now and then I would steal a glance in their direction as I trotted along on my rounds. Ledyard himself was everywhere, directing the defense and encouraging the men. He had shucked his coat and hat, for it was middling warm, but he cut a splendid figure all the same as he strode, sword in hand, up and down the rows of toiling gunners.

I heard one of Halsey's crew shout, "Their colonel's down!" And I could not resist peering over the wall. Eyre was on the ground, a knot of officers clustered around him. I learned later that he died there on the western slope, but my view of the event was cut short when a volley of musket fire whizzed over my head, and I suddenly recalled that I had business elsewhere. I went back to rolling out kegs of powder.

Our guns took their toll. But the Reg'lars kept coming on. It was a fearful sight, I can tell ye, to see that solid wall of red moving steadily up on two sides of us. Time and again, we'd cut loose at 'em, bowling over dozens at a crack. But our cannon were too few, and their numbers too great. Our men, sweat as they might, just could not load and fire fast enough to stem the oncoming scarlet tide. If only they had come at us from due west, as Ledyard had said, we'd have blown the lot of 'em clean into the river. As it was, our main battery was good for nothing, and most of the men were obliged to satisfy themselves with picking off a redcoat here and there with their muskets.

Major Montgomery was now at the very gates of the Fort. One of his men attempted to force the lock, but he was knocked over by one of our sharpshooters. The British musketry was pouring in now, rattling like hail off the barracks' walls. A chance shot from one of their field pieces cut through the halyard of our flagstaff, and I saw our beautiful stars and stripes go fluttering to the grass. Young Luke Perkins dropped his musket and dashed out to retrieve the fallen flag. Seemingly unmindful of the lead humming in at him, he fastened our banner to a pikestaff and set it firmly in the ground. It was about as stirring and noble a thing as I ever hope to see, and we all cheered Luke like mad.

Six or eight of our men were down by this time, wounded or dead — or dying. I saw Nathan Moore go down, roll over, and lie still. Dan Eldridge was sitting on the ground near the well, nursing a shattered knee; Stephen Hempstead, Shapley's first sergeant at Fort Trumbull, had his blood-soaked handkerchief wound round his head, but he was still on his feet, directing the fire from his little nine-pounder. As I came jogging out of the magazine, nearly doubled over under the weight of a bag of shot, I saw Youngs Ledyard bending over Captain Moore. Suddenly, he straightened, flung his arms high, and fell across the body of his fallen friend.

I was sick and scared clean through, but there wasn't time to weep, and there was no place to hide. God knows, if there had been, I was of a mind to fly. But I couldn't run and I couldn't rest; I had to keep humping powder and shot. How I kept going, I can't say. I was soaked in sweat, half-blind from smoke and nearly deafened by the roar of the guns. My heart was pounding fit to burst, and my whole body ached and trembled.

I was coming up on Father's position, staggering under the weight of my load, when I saw the men fall back and grab for their weapons. Montgomery's men had broken through! They were coming in over the wall!

I dropped my bag and turned tail, meaning to take cover in one of the barracks; but, to my horror, I saw that the Reg'lars were swarming up the southwest rampart, too. Our cannon were no good to us now. It was swords and pikes and muskets at close range, between two divisions of British troops and a handful of half-trained militia.

I saw Father and Lambo, standing back to back, blazing away with their muskets. And big Sam Edgecomb, laughing like a crazy man, was standing on the parapet hurling down eighteen-pound balls on the advancing enemy with his two bare hands. Azel Woodworth, the blood gushing from his nose and mouth, sat like a broken toy, his back braced against the brick wall of the powder house. Rufus Avery was locked in a desperate struggle with a lobsterback. I saw him use his knee to good effect, doubling his man over and sending him to the ground with a hard blow to the temple.

It was like a scene from Hell. All around me, men were cursing, struggling, shooting, dying. And I was purely paralyzed by fear. Sense told me to run, but my feet wouldn't, or couldn't. The wonder of it is that I wasn't shot dead a score of times.

Not ten yards from where I stood, Lieutenant Richard Chapman of Fort Trumbull was struck in the breast by a ball and was dead before he hit the ground. Captain Halsey was lying sprawled across the gun he had commanded so ably, and near him lay Wait Lester, staring up unseeing into a bright and cloudless noonday sky.

Father, Tom and Jordan were still on their feet, falling back a step at a time. I couldn't see Lambo anywhere, but in the noise and confusion and smoke — and my own terror-stricken state — I might not have recognized my own self in a mirror, I was that muddled.

"There's Montgomery!" I heard Captain Stanton roar. He was standing on the parapet, knee-deep in dead and dying men, and pointing to the eastern gate.

Sure enough, directly in front of Father and his men, Montgomery and his lieutenants were coming over. I saw Father ram home a charge in his musket, but before he could level his piece, Jordan, naked to the waist and glistening with sweat, took up his whaling lance and drove it through the British major's breast. A ragged volley of musket fire erupted from the ranks of the redcoats, and Jordan went down.

Something snapped in my brain then, and I broke and ran towards Father's battery, screaming, "Jordan, Jordan, Jordan!" as I ran.

I did not get far. A hand shot out, grabbed me by the hair, and flung me flat on my back. When my vision cleared, I found myself staring up into the grinning face of a British sergeant.

"Where away, ma wee laddie?" he said. "It's no time for dinner yet."

"Leave me go!" I cried, making as if to rise.

"Not just yet," said he, thrusting me back down with his foot. "I've a bit more killin' to do, then I'll tend to you."

Quite calmly, he placed one foot on my middle to hold me in place and set to loading his piece. "Don't move now, laddie," he said. "Ye mustn't spoil my aim."

There came a sharp report, and I heard him say, "Missed. God damn the luck! But we'll just — Ho-ho! What's this? What's this? There's the white flag, lad. Your commander means to surrender!

"Here. On your feet, now. I want ye to see for yourself what happens to scurvy rebels." He hauled me up on my legs and, grasping me by the back of the neck, he turned my head towards the parade.

It was suddenly deathly still, save for the cries and groans of the wounded. All firing had ceased, and I could see our men laying down their arms. Then I saw Ledyard, his head high, marching toward a knot of British officers standing hard by the well. His sword was in his hand, and as he advanced, he steadily raised and lowered it in the gesture of surrender. We had been whipped. Beaten. And now I would have to stand helplessly by and witness the final humiliation.

"Let's get closer, laddie," my captor said. "I want ye to see this and remember it all your life."

He dragged me along so close that I could see plainly the gloating smiles on the British officers' faces. Ledyard, surely aware that his own men were watching, carried himself proudly, no hint of shame or despair in his bearing. He halted before the enemy chiefs.

"That's Cap'n Bromfield, laddie," the sergeant said, "the handsome chap standin' there wi' his arms folded. He's our commander now that Eyre and Montgomery are dead."

I could not have said anything, even if there were anything to say. The tears were streaming down my face, and my heart was nigh to breaking. I heard the British captain call out, "Who is in command of the Fort?" And I remember thinking there was no need for him to shout so, with our Colonel standing right there.

Ledyard reversed his sword and, handing it to Bromfield, he said, "I was, Sir, but you are now."

Bromfield took the sword and — as God's my witness — he thrust it into Ledyard's breast.

For one brief moment, it seemed as if the world had ceased to turn, as our brains refused to take in the horror that our eyes had seen. My captor drew in his breath sharply, and I heard him whisper the Lord's name. Then I heard Amos Stanton's mighty voice ring out: "My God! Must we die so?"

I glanced up and saw him leap to the platform, take up a musket by the muzzle and lay about the Reg'lars like Samson among the Phillistines. A musket cracked, and Stanton toppled like a felled oak. His rage, however, touched off an explosion in scores of stout hearts. Our men went mad with wrath, falling upon the Reg'lars with bare hands, stones, and clubbed muskets, to avenge the murder of our gallant Colonel.

Stunned by the ferocity of the conquered, the conquerors fell back before the savage onslaught. I saw Tom Wansuc rise up out of nowhere and break a man's skull with a ramrod. Sam Edgecomb picked up one redcoat bodily and hurled him down from the platform, then wheeled and kicked another so hard in the middle that he went flying over the rampart to crash on the ground below. Everywhere I looked, men were grappling, clubbing, punching, rolling around in the dust. David Palmer opened up a man's belly with his sheath knife, and Thomas Starr was straddling a Reg'lar and hammering him into a jelly with his fists.

It was crazy, hopeless, horrible. The screaming and cursing was like the cries of the damned, and I swear ye could hear bones snap.

"Form squads, damn ye! Form squads!" roared Captain Bromfield, waving his sword and running up and down like a man gone out of his mind, trying to rally 'em to quell the uprising. A few at first, then more, drew up in some semblance of a formation, their bayonets glinting in the bright September sun.

"Laddie," growled my captor, who all this while had not let go his hold, "get out o' this. Ye've seen too much already. Run, now, ye damned little Rebel. Run! Get away!"

I was twelve. I ran.

Out of the Fort and on down the deserted road I pelted, running, running, running, my heart-beat drumming in my ears. At my back, I could hear the cracking of muskets, the screams of the dying, the hellish dreadful din of war. And though I ran faster than I'd run in all my life before, I could not out run the horrors I had seen. I see them still in dreams.

I drew up, panting and blowing, at my father's house. How still it all seemed, how desolate, deserted and strange. There was the door through which I had passed — how many times? — out to a day's frolic, or in to comfort, safety and peace. Now I stood there, like a stranger at the gate, hardly knowing whether to go in or pass by.

I hesitated, I didn't know why. But, having nowhere else to go, I at last lifted the latch and walked in. Silence. Nothing. I slunk up the stairs like a thief, stole into my tiny chamber, flung myself down on my bed, and promptly fell into a deep sleep.

I cannot understand that, even now. How could I have slept, after all I had seen that day? Many a night thereafter, I would lie and long for such a sleep as a dying man longs for water. But then, with all that horror yet fresh and vivid in my mind, I slept more soundly than a babe upon its mother's breast.

When I woke, it was nearly dusk. Long shadows edged slowly up the chamber wall. For a moment, I was confused, not knowing where I was or what I did there. Then, like a great wave rolling in from the sea, all my recollection of that awful day engulfed me. I think I cried out; I know that I rolled over, buried my face in my pillow and wept. Great wrenching sobs welled up in my breast and tore out of my throat with such force as to well nigh strangle me. I was so alone, so afraid, so terribly young.

At last I dragged myself up from my bed, and for the first time I realized that I had lost control of my bowels and bladder. Stinking, clammy, and altogether mortified, I tottered from my room and went down the stairs and out to the pump. Still sobbing, half-choked by my own stench, I filled bucket after bucket with water and carted 'em into the kitchen to fill the copper tub. I didn't bother with heating it; I just wanted to get clean.

I removed my clothes outside and left 'em in a heap on the ground; then I went in, climbed into the tub, and scrubbed myself raw.

I felt a little better then, but fearfully weak and kind of hollow. I dug out fresh clothes from the press and pulled 'em on, moving like a man trying to swim in mud. My belly felt pinched and empty, and great grumbling sounds rumbled up from within me. I had not eaten a thing since daybreak, and precious little then.

I went to the pantry, found a loaf of bread, a wedge of cheese, some cold meat and about half a pie. I wolfed down some of everything, washing down huge mouthfuls with gulps of cider straight from the jug.

It helped. I belched a few times, then went out to dispose of my soiled garments. I just picked 'em up with a spade and carried 'em out back of the barn, where I buried 'em.

Whether it was the exertion of digging or the reek of my own filth that did it, I don't know, but cheese, bread, meat, cider and pie all came up in one tremendous rush. I surely lost it all on the first heave, but I couldn't stop retching. I hurt all over, and my throat burned as if I'd swallowed lye. Lord, I was sick! I went down on all fours and just heaved and heaved, though there was nothing left to bring up.

At last the retching ceased, and I just collapsed exhausted on the grass. A cool breeze picked up, and it blew over me, soothing and kind. The fevered feeling eased away, and I began to feel my strength returning. Then, suddenly, I became aware of a familiar sound. Our cow, Beauty, was complaining that she hadn't been milked.

I dragged myself up and went to the pump. I stuck my head under and soaked myself good, then I took in a couple of gulps to rinse out my mouth, but I knew better than to swallow any. I straightened up and filled my lungs with sweet evening air, then I headed for the barn to tend to Beauty.

I drew up the stool, set the pail in place, and commenced milking. It was dark in the barn, and the good smell of hay was most welcome to my nostrils. I felt suddenly weary, and low and unspeakably sad. I rested my head against Beauty's silken flank, and just kept pulling away, not thinking, just listening to the buzz of the flies and the cheerful sound of the jets of milk hitting the sides of the pail.

I wasn't asleep, surely, but I was not properly awake either; rather, I was in a kind of trance, as ye might say, just letting my mind run on while my hands kept working.

The pleasantest kind of pictures began to take shape inside my head. I saw, or fancied that I saw, lovely blue water, with stands of green trees all around. It looked like the pond where Jordan and Tom and I had gone a-fishing that blessed evening so long ago. Thinking of them made me happy and sad at once, and I was just conscious of a tear sliding down my face. Jordan and Tom! What times we'd had. I could see their faces rising up before me in the darkness; smiling, happy faces, faces that I —

Suddenly, I felt a hand on my shoulder and, so caught up was I in my vision that I just turned around smiling and said, "Jordan?"

"No, Will. It's me."

Father!

I sprang up, upsetting the pail, and flung myself into Father's arms, hugging him hard as I could and holding so tight as if I meant never to let him go.

He rested his face on top of my head and just held me. "Billy, Billy," he said. "I been lookin' for ye, boy. I was so afraid, so afraid."

I commenced to cry. I couldn't help it. I just burrowed my face into his shirt and wept myself dry.

"Easy, Sonny, easy," he crooned. "There, there, there. It's over now. It's all over. The Reg'lars are all gone off, and you ain't hurt any, thank the Lord. Come. Let's go into the house. I've got to get some food into me, or

I'll faint on ye; and then where would ye be, hey?"

To this day, I don't know what was so funny about that, but I started in laughing, and I cackled and screeched so that a body'd a-thought I'd gone crazy. I didn't want to laugh, and I surely wanted to stop. But I couldn't stop. I fairly howled; my sides aching, and the tears flowing, and my breath coming so short that I thought I should surely die.

"Stop it, Will," said Father, sharply. "Stop it!"

I couldn't. I shook my head and just kept on gasping and howling till Father backhanded me hard across the face. The force of his blow snapped my head back and near stunned me. But it put a stop to that horrid laughter.

"I'm sorry, Will," said Father, putting his arm around me, "but you were making yourself sick."

"It — it's all right, Father," said I, rubbing my cheek. "I don't know why I was carryin' on so, but once I got started, I just couldn't stop."

Father patted my shoulder. "Come along," he said, gently. "Come along, now."

As we moved down the path to the house, Father leaned on me pretty heavily, and I became aware that he was favoring one leg. "Ye're hurt!" I cried.

"Shh-shh. 'Tis nothing. I took a ball in the thigh, is all. Dr. Downer turned up in time to take it out, and he says I'll mend as good as new."

We went into the kitchen, and Father lighted a lamp and set it down on the table. I was shocked to see how gray and drawn he looked. There were lines in his face I had not seen before, and his eyes were dark and brooding, with nothing of their former fire.

He sat down hard in his accustomed chair, his injured leg sticking out stiffly before him. "Will," he said, "we must get to your uncle's house tonight. Your poor mother will be going out of her mind with worry. But I got to clean up first. I can't have her seein' me like this,"

"I'll heat the water for ye, Father," said I, glad of the chance to do something for him. "And I'll see if I can't scare ye up somethin' to eat."

"Will?"

"Yes, Sir?"

"Come here, boy. That's it. Fine." Father rubbed his eyes and blinked a few times, then he gazed directly at me and said, "Will, you know, don't ye, that Jordan is dead?"

There it was. I had known it, the way you can know a thing even if you haven't proved it for yourself. I guess I knew when Jordan fell that he'd never get up again. But I had pretended to believe that he was only wounded; that someone would find him and patch him up and put him on his legs once more. I needed to believe that. I had to. And so I made myself believe that I believed.

"It's all right to cry if ye want to, Will," Father said, so gently that I was nearly moved to tears by his kindness. "It ain't unmanly to weep for a friend."

I shook my head. "I — I guess I'm all cried out, Father," I said. And it was so. Much as I grieved for Jordan, and for myself at losing him, I had no tears left to shed.

"I can understand that," Father said. "Reckon Jordan would, too. He was an uncommonly good friend to ye, Billy. I guess he'd not want ye to take this too much to heart."

"I loved Jordan, Father."

"I know that, boy. He loved you, too."

I shook my head to clear my brain. "I'll be a long time mournin' him, Father. An awful long time. But I just can't cry anymore."

Father patted my arm. "There'll be a time for it, Will. It says so in the Book. 'To every thing there is a season, and a time to every purpose under the heaven . . . a time to weep . . . and a time to mourn. . . .' "

He sighed heavily, then he smiled and said, "I guess ye must just wait for the time. I'm certain Jordan won't mind."

I nodded, dumb.

"Now, if you'll heat the water, I'd be very much obliged."

I scurried about, building up the fire and filling the great kettle. Then I made another raid on the pantry and heaped up every scrap I could find onto a tin plate and brought it to Father. It was a pretty poor looking jumble of victuals, I guess, but Father thanked me as heartily as if I'd brought him a smoking roast beef.

"And I'll thank you for some cider, Will. My throat's wonderful dry."

I fetched the jug, then pulled up a stool and sat alongside him, while he cleaned his plate.

"Whew!" he sighed, when he'd polished off the last crumb. "That was fine! We are mighty lucky, Will, mighty lucky indeed."

"How so, Father?"

"Look around ye, boy. Here's our house, standing just as we left it. We've got food in our bellies, and we can be sure the family's safe and well." Father nodded. "Yessir, there's lots of poor souls not far from here as would give what they have to be in our place tonight."

I had to allow he was right, but I confess it came as pretty cold comfort. My mind was too full of ugliness to leave room for gratitude.

"Well, now," said Father, getting stiffly to his feet, "Reckon I'd better have my bath."

While he was scrubbing, I got out fresh clothes for him, then I came and sat down by the tub to keep him company.

"Guess we have to talk about it, don't we, Will?" he said, soaping up his neck and ears.

"Yes, Sir," I said.

"Well, suppose you tell me your story. Then I'll tell ye mine, and that'll be that. We'll just leave it here in this room. I'll do the tellin' when we join up with Mother and the gals — such tellin' as I must. Understood?"

"Yes, Sir."

"Now, then. You start."

I told him everything. He didn't say much, only grunted now and then. But he listened, and he heard me out.

Then he said, "I'm forever beholden to that redcoat for givin' ye your chance, Will. I truly am."

"But — I ran, Father. I just turned tail and ran."

"Why wouldn't ye?" Father sluiced water all over his chest and arms. "My land, boy, don't ye think we'd all have run if we could have? And don't ye know some did? You've nothin' to be ashamed of, Billy. Not one blamed thing. You came to the Fort, which is more'n some can say, and you stuck to your task as long as there was a task to do.

"You needn't feel no shame, boy. Just be thankful to the Almighty that ye got away with a whole skin. Nobody'd fault ye for it, least of all me. You showed yourself a Latham today, Will. And I'm proud of you."

Then I had to tell him about soiling my pants.

He didn't laugh. And he didn't look disgusted. He said, "Why, Billy, that happens all the time in battle. To grown men, too. I hope you don't think ye're the only one who — well, never mind. I can see ye're mortified just talkin' about it. But you may take my word for it, it happens to the bravest and the best."

Well I felt better for having told him, though I could hardly believe that real soldiers ever had that happen to 'em. I was very young.

Father got out of the tub, dried himself and got dressed. I had to help him get his breeches on over his hurt leg, but otherwise he managed very well.

"Now, Billy," he said, settling into his chair, "I have to tell ye some things that ain't too pleasant. But I think I must get 'em said. And as you were there, you have right to know — a right, and a duty, too. For you must remember all o' this, remember what we suffered and why."

"Yes, Sir."

"Well, it was purely a massacre. There's no other word for it. Once the Reg'lars got themselves together again, they just went after us with murder in their hearts. They were shootin' and stabbin' and clubbin' as if they meant to kill us all. Indeed, they did mean to. But their own officers was so sick at the slaughter that they finally called a halt to it — but not before a good many of our neighbors lay dead."

Father paused, remembering, his eyes staring off at scenes he alone could see. "The Colonel was already dead, of course. And Youngs Ledyard, too, and Halsey and Stanton and about nine or ten Averys. And Lambo's dead. Did I tell ye Lambo's dead, Will?"

"No, Father."

"Ay-uh." He sniffed loudly. "He kept up fightin' to the last, but a ball took him clean through the brain. He didn't suffer none, Will. I promise ye that. He had no pain at the last."

I just shut my eyes and steeled myself to hear him out.

"Oh, Lord, Billy, I can scarce remember all that was killed. Chesters and Allyns, most of the Perkins boys — Luke and Elnathan and Asa, Simeon and 'Lisha, too, all dead.

"I dunno, Billy. I dunno how this town's

ever goin' to recover from this day. I keep thinkin' we should have listened to Amos Stanton. But how was we to know? We thought — we thought help was comin'. But they never showed. They never showed."

Father frowned, and his eyes went hard and cold. "I'd give a deal to know what become of Benadam Gallup and his reinforcements. Damn, boy! I'd purely love to know.

"Where was I? Well, when the firin' ceased, the redcoats gave us a taste o' their brand o' mercy. They piled the most gravely wounded into an ammunition cart — about thirty-five of us, all told, defenseless, bleedin' men. Their comrades went about the field, stripping the bodies of our dead, while others marched off with thirty or so sound men to make prisoners of them aboard one their ships.

"Rufus Avery was carried off, and Dan Eldridge, though he was bad hurt, and Josiah Smith, and I don't know who all. They are pris'ners tonight, Will, chained in the stinking hold of an enemy ship."

Father reached for his pipe, charged it with 'baccy and lit up. Then he said, "Squire Ledyard's a pris'ner, too, Will."

"The Squire! But he's an old man, Father. He wasn't in the fightin' or —"

"True, true, as ye say. But that grand old man, in the midst of his own grief for his son and his brother, when he heard there was some wounded among the prisoners being carried off, he came down from his big house and offered to go as hostage on their stead. And he's gone, Will, a prisoner with the rest." Father shook his head in admiration. "There ain't a man in the whole of England worthy to black Eben Ledyard's shoes.

"Well, Sir, there we was lyin' in that cart, stacked like cordwood and helpless as babes. Some of the men was dyin', and some was screamin' in their pain. And anytime somebody moved, somebody else got hurt some more.

"I was dumped right on top, luckily, and next to me lay that Injun friend o' Jordan's —"

"Tom! Tom Wansuc. Is he alive, Father? Oh, tell me Tom's alive!"

"Why, certain he is, boy. He walked back to the Fort with me this evenin' to help identify the dead."

My heart swelled to bursting. Tom at least had been spared!

"He got stuck in the neck with a bayonet. Lucky for him, he looked far worse'n he felt, otherwise they'd have took him off with Rufus Avery and the rest. But he was all over blood, and he played 'possum so well that they must have reckoned him all but gone.

"Anyway, when them scavengers was

through with pickin' over our dead, they came over to the cart and cussed us all roundly for makin' so much noise. God A'mighty! If ever devils walked the earth, they wore red coats, I promise ye.

"Billy, they took a chain and fastened it to the cart. They dragged it to the top of the hill, and then they sprang aside and just let it go, rollin' faster and faster down towards the river!

"How that cart traveled! It was well weighted, ye see, with its torn and bleedin' load, and it went plummetin' down like a thunderbolt, jouncin' over the stones and woundin' the wounded more." Father shuddered and passed his hand over his eyes. "I can hear the screamin' still.

"I reckoned it was all up with us. I figgered they'd find us floatin' in the mornin'. But, as luck would have it, that cart ran smack dab into the big apple tree near Ebenezer Avery's place, flipped over, and spilled us out on the ground."

"Were any killed, Father?"

"It's hard to say. Some may have already been dead afore we hit, Will. Some, it may be, died in the crash. However it was, Tom Wansuc and me, and one or two others as could get about fairly well, dragged our comrades into Avery's house. His missus was there, and his gals. They took hold, and by the time the Downers turned up with their medical kits, the men had all been bathed and tended to, and we was about as comfortable as we could be in the circumstances.

"Joshua Downer got 'round to me in good time, and he cut that ball out just as neat as ye please, and bound me up, and said he reckoned I'd live to be a hunnert."

"I hope so, Father," I said.

He smiled at that and said, "As the Lord wills, boy." He lay his pipe aside and, rubbing his chin thoughtfully, he said, "There ain't much more to tell. That big Injun and I and some others went back up to the Fort afore sundown. The redcoats had carried off their dead, o' course, so we was in possession of the Fort once more, in a manner o' speakin'.

"We counted eighty-four bodies, Will. Eighty-four! More'n half of those that stood with us this mornin' are standin' before their Maker tonight."

He rubbed his forehead as if it pained him, then he said, "There was about a score of 'em in the magazine. They'd fled there when the massacre began, and they died there, shot like so many sittin' ducks.

"It was dreadful, Billy, dreadful! All them fine men and boys cut down like that." He shielded his eyes with his hand, but not before

I saw a tear trace its way down his stubbled cheek.

I put my hand on his arm and said, "Father, I'm awful glad you wa'n't killed."

His strong fingers closed over mine and squeezed 'em hard. "Thank'ee, Will," he said. "I hope that I shall be glad o' that myself, in time. Tonight, well, it's hard, boy, awful hard, to find much comfort in bein' alive in a town where so many of the best are dead."

"Don't say so, Father!" I cried. "You said yourself we was lucky and ought to be thankful."

"So I did; so I did."

"Well, we are lucky. And I am thankful. We — we need ye, Father, Mother and Luke and the gals and me. We couldn't none of us stand it if you was to be taken from us. I know I couldn't."

Father drew me over close to him and hugged me to his side. "You could stand it, Billy, better'n most. But I am glad after all that ye don't have to. Ye lost a great deal in losin' your friend; it wouldn't be right for you to have to lose a father, too."

"Did — did Jordan say anything, Father? Before he died?"

Father shook his head. "I wish I could tell you anything that'd give ye comfort, Will, but the truth of it is, I was so fearful busy that

I wouldn't have heard him if he did. I — well, I think he was likely killed outright. Chances are he never said a word."

I nodded, swallowing hard. "He was awful brave, wasn't he, Father?"

"Brave? I should say so! Why, Billy, he stood up to 'em like a reg'lar hero. I never had a better man serve under me. He was so quick and strong and cheerful. If we'd had a hunnert more like him, I guess it would have been a different story I'd be tellin' ye now. Yessir, you can be mighty proud o' your friend Jordan, boy. He was a fine soldier and a fine man."

"I — I shall miss him somethin' fierce, Father."

"I know ye will, boy. I know ye will." Father patted my shoulder. "There ain't nothin' anybody can say or do to take away your hurt, but if there was, ye know I'd move heaven and earth to do it. I have lost friends, too; good friends. And I know there just ain't nothin' that'll make the hurtin' stop, except time, mebbe, and forgettin'."

"I won't ever forget Jordan," I said.

"No, no. 'Course ye won't. I didn't mean forgettin', exactly. Only that you will, in time, forget the ugly parts and the pain, and start to rememberin' him as he was." Father smiled up at me. "Mem'ries are a great blessin', Will.

They're a way for keepin' them that we loved alive and with us always."

"Father?"

"Ay-uh?" he said, absently stroking my hair.

"Father, thank you for — for talkin' to me."

Tears brimmed in his eyes, but he spoke up briskly, "Je-rusalem, boy! I'm your pa, ain't I?"

"Yes, Sir," I said, smiling. "Yes, Sir. And I'm awful glad."

His lips twitched then, and he winked and said, "Me, too."

"Would ye care for some more cider, Father?"

"I'd rather have about a week's sleep," he said. "I'm weary, boy. And I hurt in places I'd forgot I had. But we must get to your mother, or she'll never forgive us. Reckon she'll bless you out some as 'tis, but don't you mind it none. A mother's got some rights, I guess, and you'll just have to stand it as best ye can."

He pushed himself up out of his chair, and we walked out into the cool night air. Our team hadn't come home, and where they could be was anybody's guess. So I had to go out to the back lot and bring in the shaggy old plough horse, Abner. He was about as big as a mountain, but gentle as a tabby cat. He nickered to me as I came up to him in the dark, and he followed along meek as a lamb to the shed. Father and I hitched him up to the ratty old shay that had been weathering out there for as long as I could remember, then we climbed in and Father took the reins.

" 'Tain't what ye'd call a stylish rig," he said, "but I guess it'll get us where we mean to go. Git along, Abner. Gee-up!"

It was soothing somehow just to be rolling through the night. A half-moon was shining, and there was just a hint of autumn in the wind. Crickets were tuning up their fiddles in the high grass, and from far off in the black-shadowed woods, we heard a screech owl take up her doleful refrain.

"Father?" said I, huddling closer to him as we entered Dark Hollow Woods.

"Yes, Will?"

"There's somethin' I have to ask of ye. It — it's for Jordan, mainly, but it would be a great favor to me, too."

"A favor, hey?" Father sniffed. "Well, I don't know but what you have one comin' to ye, Will. Try me."

And I told him about Sally.

He was silent for a good while, then he said, "And she's goin' to have his child, ye say?"

"Yes, Sir. And, well, I know Jordan was mighty set on havin' his child born free. If

— if you could buy Sally away from Colonel Harris, then she could be free and keep her baby — hers and Jordan's; and I just know that Jordan would know it somehow and be glad."

"Ye-es. Yes, I expect he would."

"I'd be glad to put up my wages, Father. And I'd be more'n willin' to pay ye back the balance as I can."

"That's fair enough," said Father. "Can't see any flaws in that arrangement. But, Will, it'll take you a dreadful long time to pay me off, ye know, and it won't leave ye with much for your own spendin'."

"I don't care about that," I said. "I just want Jordan's child born free."

"Hum. Well, tell ye what. You put up your wages, as ye said. And I'll take care o' the balance myself. That way, I don't deprive you of the chance to do somethin' for Jordan, and it gives me a chance to do somethin' for him — and for you."

"Oh, Father," I said, "that's awful handsome of you."

"Well, Billy, I never did get to free poor Lambo. And I do feel obliged to Jordan on more'n one account. This way, mebbe I can square my conscience some. I never did like carryin' debts.

"Soon as things settle down some, I'll make

it my business to git across to New London — what's left of it — and look up Harris. I reckon I know how to work a bargain out of that old skinflint."

I settled back on the mouldy seat and just stared up at the faint sprinkling of pale stars. Somewhere, way out beyond the farthest star, lay Heaven, where Jesus sits upon a golden throne to judge them that have died. I thought of Jordan standing there, tall and proud, a free man who had fallen in Freedom's cause. And I knew. Right down inside my soul I knew that Jesus would let Jordan Freeman in.

"Yonder's your uncle's house, Will," said my father, his voice bringing me out of my reverie. "See they kept a lamp burnin' for us."

"Git along, Abner!" I said, snapping my fingers at the steady old plodder. "Git along, now!"

Father chuckled. "Feel as though ye could stand to see folks now?"

"Yes, Sir," I said. "And glad to."

CHAPTER XV

There followed a doleful time for us all. The whole countryside was in mourning. Hardly a home was there that had not been touched by the scourge of battle, and for a time it seemed that life was nothing but a procession of funerals as we set about the work of burying our dead.

The spirit had gone out of our village, not only because of the general woe, but because of the bitter recrimination leveled at those who had failed to come to the Fort. Poor Nathan Gallup went about under a cloud, though it was later determined before a court-martial that he was in no way to blame for not showing. He had ridden clear to Lebanon, alerted Governor Trumbull, and, borrowing a fresh mount, had come flying back as fast as he could. But by the time he reached the outskirts of New London, why, the waterfront was already in flames, and there was no way for him to get across to the Groton side.

As for his older brother, Benadam, I judge that he must have lived out his days as the loneliest man in Groton. He explained, to any who would listen, that he had indeed tried to rouse the countryside, but that when the men drew near the Fort, they just turned around and lit out for home. The old soldier was himself none too spry, and with the enemy so near, there wasn't anyway he could have got back into the Fort on his own. So he did the sensible thing; he retreated and lived. But Benadam was a broken man. Most shunned him; most damned him for a coward and a traitor. They say if he'd have been a real officer, he'd have been cashiered for sure.

I don't know. I don't believe that old Benadam was either a coward or a traitor. I believe it happened just as he said. Some of them that spoke the hardest words against him had been pretty scarce that day themselves. Benadam Gallup was, after all, an old man, and he had tried to do something helpful. There are men a good deal younger and a whole lot healthier walking around these parts who didn't attempt so much. It would become them, I think, to hold their peace.

I came down sick a day or two after the battle. Dr. Prentiss was afraid I'd taken the brain fever. But, as Lucy said afterward, he needn't have worried none because I hadn't any brain anyway. Whatever it was, it knocked me off my feet for a week and more. I was feverish, brain or no brain, and there were times when I was out of my head and raving.

Father told me later that sometimes he had to just about sit on me to hold me down in the bed. What's worse, he told me that while I was out of my head my language got pretty brisk, and Mother heard things she never expected to hear coming from me. Father said I seemed to think I was back at the Fort, and that I was blessing out the enemy in terms no one could fail to understand. I felt pretty cheap, saying such things in front of Mother, but she never spoke to me about it, and I was grateful.

About the time the sickness went off and I was able to come downstairs again and sit by the window to watch the leaves turn, Father found his first opportunity to get across to New London. And I almost made myself sick all over again, just waiting and fidgeting and sweating till he returned.

We had agreed, he and I, that this matter of Sally was our private business, and we kept it to ourselves, excluding even Mother.

"It ain't that I mean to have secrets from her, Will," Father had said, "But the truth is, she has been after me for so blessed long to buy a decent rig for ridin' out to church and visitin' and such that she might not take kindly to my layin' out money for another purpose. Let's just trim our sails and hold to our course till we know where matters stand. There'll be time for explanations afterward, I'm certain."

Father came in about suppertime, and of course the whole family was on deck, so he had no chance to say a private word to me. Mother and the gals were so full of questions that he had all he could to sneak in a mouthful of food between replies.

New London, he said, was a shambles. Near two hundred buildings had gone up — the warehouses along the beach, the church, the courthouse, and more than sixty houses.

"It's a sight to freeze the marrow," Father declared. "I never saw such devastation."

"What about Colonel Harris's house, Father?" said I, all innocence.

"Spared," he said, shooting me a warning glance. "They say that Arnold ascended to the summit o' Town Hill to enjoy the whole proceedin's. Damn his eyes!"

"Will!" said my mother.

"Well," he growled, "I can't help it. When I think o' that — that turncoat comin' back to his own region and reducin' a whole town to ashes while his troops run riot among the people, it just sticks in my throat. It does, truly."

He tore savagely at the hunch of bread in

his hand. "It ain't for me to question the Almighty, I know; but how a just God could let William Ledyard die and that renegade live is more'n I can fathom."

" 'Vengeance is mine, saith the Lord,' Will," said Mother. "You must leave it to him."

He crammed a great hunk of bread into his mouth and chewed furiously, his face red, the veins in his forehead standing out as if they were about to burst. "It's wrong dammit. And when I die I mean to ask the Lord the why of it, if I go to Hell for askin'."

"Will, please. The children —"

"All right, Mother, all right. I didn't mean to upset ye. It's just that seein' all that — that wreckage today got me so het up that I can scarcely stand it." He wiped his mouth on the back of his hand and rose from the table.

"Will," he said, "there's somethin' I have to talk to you about out to the barn. You feelin' fit to go so far?"

"Yes, Father."

"Well, then, get your hat and coat. It's coolish, and I don't want ye to take cold."

I donned my things and followed Father out to the barn. He lit a lantern, then seated himself on an upturned pail. "Draw up the milkin' stool, Will," he said. "Drat! Where's my 'baccy? Oh. There 'tis."

He made a great business of stuffing his pipe and getting it going to his satisfaction.

"There now," said he, leaning forward, his elbows on his knees, "I do favor a pipe after I've et. Seems to help things settle somehow."

"Father, did ye get to talk to Colonel Harris?"

"Not directly. I got to his house all right, but I never got to talk to him. He ain't showin' his face these days, Will, and with reason." Father spat into the straw that littered the floor. "He's in trouble, Will. Bad trouble."

"How so, Father?"

"He run from the enemy, boy. He just purely upped and run. I got it from friends in New London, good honest men that ain't never lied so long as I've known 'em. And that's been a while, I promise ye."

Father puffed hard on his pipe for a bit, then he said, "It happened this way, Will. When the British moved in on the town, some of the men turned out with such weapons as they had and rallied around the old field piece atop Town Hill. They had no leader and no real plan, but they had courage. They meant to do some damage, whatever the cost to themselves.

"Well, Sir, while they was standin' there pow-wowin' amongst themselves, who should come riding by but Colonel Harris. The enemy was by this time in plain view, and you can bet them New Londoners was glad to see Harris.

"One of 'em says, 'Colonel, now we have someone to command us, and we are at your service.'

"And d'ye know what Harris said, Will? D'ye know what he said to those men?"

"No, Sir."

"He said," and here Father's voice took on a horrible mincing tone, "he said, 'Ye must excuse me, gentlemen, as I have a violent sick headache this morning and can hardly sit my horse.'

"And he turned his horse and rode off.

"Je-rusalem, boy, but them fellers was hoppin' mad! Nate Saltonstall told me that one of the men — and a very respectable man, too; I know him, but I won't say his name — cocked his piece and leveled it at Harris's back, sayin', 'Let's shoot the damned rascal!'

"And he would have, too, and done right in doin' it, only Saltonstall stopped him."

Father spat again into the straw. "Colonel Harris! If that's what they call a colonel, then God help us. I'm glad they didn't shoot him, for I want to be there when he's hanged."

I don't know when I'd seen Father so wrought up. His eyes were snapping, and his voice fairly crackled.

"Well," he said, more calmly now, though I could see his hands were shaking, "we had a colonel at any rate, didn't we, Will? Yessir, by Godfrey, we had a colonel to be proud of. But he's dead, and that — that bag of suet will probably get off and live out a long, useless life in that big house o' his. Much good may it do him."

"Father," said I, "what about Sally?"

"I was just comin' to that," he said, rubbing his jaws and staring up into the blackness of the hayloft.

I waited.

At last he lowered his gaze and, looking directly at me, he said, "She's gone, Will."

"Gone? Where?"

He shook his head. "I dunno. Harris's servant come to the door, and I ast him could I talk to his master. He said Harris was sick a-bed and couldn't see anybody. Well, I knew that was a damned lie, but I let it slide for the moment, and I ast him where was Sally. He told me she'd been sold off, Billy. I'm awful sorry."

Hopelessness came over me like a cloud. I could not have defined despair, but I felt it. I just sat there, whipped, dumb, defeated.

"I ast him who she was sold to, Billy, but he didn't know. I don't think he lied. He really didn't know. He had taken refuge over to Quaker Hill and had only got back lately; Sally was gone afore he got back, and the colonel was speakin' to no one."

Father reached out and took hold of my hand. "I tried, Billy. I did try. I sought a word with Missus Harris, poor distraught creetur. She come to the door, her eyes all puffed and red with weepin'. I felt as much pity for her as I felt contempt for her husband.

"She could tell me nothin'. She'd fled the town, too, but Sally got left back somehow, and Harris had sold her off afore his missus come back. She said he was so sick now that he couldn't talk, and there was nothin' to be learned by confrontin' him.

"I figger what we must do is bide our time for a bit, and then, when Harris gives it out that he's feelin' better, why I'll just go over there and —"

"It's all right, Father," I said. "It ain't any use anyway. She's gone. And now I can't ever do what I meant to do for Jordan."

"Billy, Billy, ye can't just give it up. Not you. You ain't made that way. I know it."

But I did give up. My heart was just worn out with grieving and caring. It looked to me like nothing could ever go right anymore, and there was no use in my trying to make it go right, because it just wasn't to be.

I felt bad for Father. I could see that he was trying every way he could to make me hope. But I was fresh out. I just couldn't hope anymore. I got up on my legs and said, "I thank ye for what ye did, Father. I guess I better go in now. I — I'm feelin' kind of peaked."

Father rose and put his arm around me. " 'Course ye are," he said. "You had a terrible fever, Will. You must be plumb wore out. Come along now. You get a good night's rest and tomorrow, why, things'll look ever so much brighter. You'll see."

I knew it wasn't so, but I didn't argue. I was too tired, too sick, too miserable to care. I just let him steer me back to the house. All I wanted was sleep and forgetting. It didn't matter to me if I ever waked again.

A day slid by, and another, and another. They were all just a blur to me. I woke, did my chores, ate, slept, and woke again. But I might as well have been dead for all the notice I paid to anyone or anything around me.

Father tried, he tried ever so hard to rouse me out of my stupor. Looking back, I marvel at the patience of the man. He had sorrows of his own sufficient to stagger even so strong a man as he was, but he was ever gentle, ever kind, trying by every means he could think of to draw me out of my melancholy. I was sensible of what he was doing, of what he was trying to do, and I ached to be able to respond. But I couldn't.

Mother fussed and fretted and declared she was going to send for Dr. Prentiss again, but Father must have talked to her, for she left off her fretting and only watched me with a careful, worried eye. My sisters, after trying their best to cheer me, finally washed their hands of the whole matter and left me alone to feed on my bitter portion of grief.

Then, one bright blue afternoon in the last week of September, when the sun was brighter than ever it is in June, and the wind was chasing the cloud flock across the pastures of the sky, Mother came and rapped on the door of my garret chamber.

"What is it?" said I, none too sweetly, for I had come away up there for solitude and had no wish to see even my mother's blessed face.

She opened the door a crack and said, "Billy? Someone's at the front door askin' for ye."

"Tell 'em I'm ill," I said. "I ain't of a mind to play."

"I don't think he's come to play with you," said Mother. "He's a mite too old for that, I guess."

"Who is it?"

"That Injun, Tom Wansuc."

"Tom?"

"Yes. He asked most 'specially if he might have a word with you. D'ye want me to send him away?"

I hadn't seen Tom since I fled the Fort. I had thought about him, of course. But I had been down with the fever, and then, when I'd learned about Sally's being sold off, well, I just forgot about Tom, and about everybody and everything — excepting my own self and my own misery.

I was almost brought out of it, just knowing that Tom had come to see me, and I felt almost cheerful as I came down the stairs. I went through the dim and sacred parlor and out into the bright afternoon, my eyes squinting against the unaccustomed light.

"How do, Billy?" said a familiar voice.

Shading my eyes, I looked up to see Tom leaning against the fence. He looked fine. He had on a handsome deerskin hunting shirt and fringed leggings. A scarlet handkerchief hid the bandage on his neck, and a fur cap crowned his glossy crow's-wing hair. I had never seen Tom dressed so before, but I liked it.

"Ye look good, Tom," I said, gaping up at him.

"You don't," he said, folding his arms

on his breast and eyeing me up and down. "They said you was sick. I guess they didn't lie."

I had to fight down an urge to just fling myself on him and weep. "I — I been poorly, Tom," I said. "I'm better now."

He held out his hand, and it made me feel stronger just to touch it. "I'd a-come sooner, Billy," he said, "but I was feelin' none too fine myself. And I doubted you was up to seein' company."

"I'm always glad to see you, Tom."

He nodded. "Me, too, Wildcat."

"Tom, you know Sally's been sold off?"

"Has she?"

"Ay-uh. I had it arranged with my father to go and buy her free — for — for Jordan. He went over to Harris's place, but they gave it out that he was sick and couldn't see anybody. And they said Sally was sold, Tom. Sold and gone, and they couldn't say where!"

Tom placed a strong hand on my shoulder. "Your pa did that, did he?"

"Yes."

He shook his head. "Boy, you have got a pa."

"He tried, Tom. But it — it wasn't any use." I blinked hard to hold back the tears. "I wanted that so."

"I know," Tom said. "It's what Jordan wanted."

The tears started to slip through, and I had to look away.

"Hey, Billy," Tom said, "take a little walk with me down to the road. There's somethin' I got to show ye."

I just nodded, for I couldn't speak, and I fell in alongside him and walked with him out to the roadway. Suddenly, Tom slipped one hand over my eyes. "No peepin', now," he said. "I'll steer ye along, but you mustn't look until — Now!"

His hand dropped away, and there before me stood a handsome spanking new wagon, drawn by a team of sturdy bays. And seated on the wagon, smiling down on me in a way that made my knees go weak, was Jordan's Sally.

My face must have been something to behold. Even Tom laughed right out loud. Then he said, "Better shut your jaw, Billy, or some squirrel will make his nest in there."

I shook my head and blinked, but she didn't go away. She was really there, Sally, smiling down at me just as real and warm as life itself.

"Hello, Billy Latham," she said.

"H-how do, Sally?" I gabbled. "I'm awful glad to see ye. I — Father said ye was sold off. I never — I don't —"

Tom Wansuc caught me under the arms and swung me up beside Sally. Her eyes seemed sad, and very old, but her smile was brighter even than the sun, and warmer. She took my hand in hers and said, "I wasn't sold, Billy. I was bought free."

"You're free?"

She nodded.

"But who — I mean, Father was — That is, we were —"

"I bought her free, Billy," Tom Wansuc said. "I just went over to New London and caught that old Harris by the throat and told him I'd come to make him the best bargain he'd ever be a party to. And I guess he believed me, because he handed over the papers without a murmur, took his money, and ran upstairs to hide under the bed."

"Ye didn't threaten him, did ye, Tom?"

Tom's eyes didn't change, but I could see the corners of his mouth curl ever so slightly. "No, Billy, I didn't threaten him. I just told him there was some men askin' around for him, and I kind of hinted that mebbe I'd be willin' to take him to see 'em, if he was of a mind to go.

"He said he wasn't."

I grinned. And it felt so good to be grinning that I just kept on till I thought my face would split. "Jordan would have liked that, Tom.

He surely would have liked that."

Tom grunted. "I guess so," he said. "He thought less of Harris than most."

"Je-rusalem!" I said, turning to Sally. "Now that baby'll be born a free man, just like Jordan wanted."

"Yes, Billy," Sally said, her eyes going misty and damp. "He'll be a free man, like his pa."

I sobered then, felling all over solemn and sad. "I wish — I wish —"

Sally nodded. "I know, Billy. I know." Then she smiled a smile so brave and sweet that it hurt my heart to see it.

"I'm mighty glad to see you well, Billy," she said. "Tom told me you was in the fightin' and everything. I'm just so thankful you wasn't hurt none."

"Me, too."

"Did you — did you see Jordan? I mean, before — ?"

"I saw him," I said. "He was mighty brave, Sally. My father says that Jordan's just about the bravest man he ever knew."

Tears welled up in Sally's eyes. "I wish he'd been a coward, Billy. I purely do."

"Hush, Sally," said Tom, his voice rough but kindly. "You mustn't fret yourself. You got to think of that baby now."

"Yes," said I, grateful to Tom for having put me in mind of it, "that will be somethin', won't it, Sally?"

She tried to smile, but it wouldn't come through. "If the baby had a father —" She could not go on.

"Hey, now, Sally," said Tom, reaching up and taking hold of her arm, "we been all over that. I told ye I'd look after you and the child."

"Will ye, Tom?" I cried. "Will ye truly?"

"Reckon I must," Tom said. "Jordan would ha'nt me all my days if I was to fail to look after his woman and his child."

"Oh, Tom! Sally! Oh, Je-rusalem, but I'm glad!" My heart fairly bounded up into my throat. "I'll help, too. You'll see. And when that baby gets here, why, I can come visit ye and help around the house and all, and we can —"

"Billy."

"Yes, Tom?"

"Billy, we ain't goin' to be your neighbors."

"Ye ain't? But — but, why, Tom? You have your house right over —"

"No, boy." Tom put his hand on my knee and looked up at me with those glittering eyes. "Sally and me, we talked it all out, and we've decided we're movin' on."

"But why, Tom? Where'll ye go that's any better'n right here?"

"Billy, I can't stay on here. What friends

I had are all dead; the best friend I'll ever have is dead. There ain't nothin' for me here."

"But I'm your friend, Tom. Ain't I?" The tears were starting; I couldn't help it, ashamed as I was to cry in front of Sally.

Tom reached up and grabbed my shoulders and squeezed hard. "You are my friend, Billy Latham. You surely are. I'll fight the man who says it ain't so. But, Billy, you — you're young, and you got a different kind of life waiting for ye. Me, I don't belong here no more. My own people are about all gone off. It — it just ain't my home anymore. You see that, don't ye?"

I couldn't speak for the sobs that swelled my throat. I only sat there shaking my head. No, no, no.

Sally slipped her arms around me and drew my head to her breast. "Billy, Billy," she said, her voice soft and warm as a southerly wind, "hush, now. It ain't that we want to leave you. Truly, that ain't so. But we mean to make a life for the baby; and, well, Billy, it won't be easy here."

"We're headin' west, Billy," Tom said, "across the Alleghenies. I mean to find me a piece of land and farm it, and just stay clear of towns and troubles and other men's wars from now on. I've had my fill of all o' that."

I mopped at my cheeks with my fists and

straightened up. "You really mean it, don't ye, Tom?"

"Yes, Billy. I do."

I nodded, swallowing hard, and feeling an awful lump where my heart used to be. "Well, then," I said, "I'll come see ye when I'm grown."

"Would ye, Billy? Would ye do that?"

"Certain I would, Tom, if ye'll have me."

"If — ? D'ye hear that, Sally? *If* we'll have him." Tom's strong bronzed face softened into a real smile. "Listen, Wildcat. You come soon and stay long, whenever ye've a mind to. We got to show that baby the kind of boy we mean for him to grow into, don't we?"

"Ye want him to be — like me?"

"He'd better be," Tom said, "or I'll lift his hair and sell what's left for fishbait. He can't have a name like Billy and not live up to it, I promise ye."

"Billy?" I turned, wide-eyed, to Sally. "Ye ain't goin' to call him Billy?"

Sally smiled and nodded. "He'll be William Jordan Freeman, if he is a he."

I never knew a prouder moment in my life. And I don't expect to, ever. "I'll come see him," I said. "I surely will."

Tom swung me down then, and he climbed up beside Sally on the seat. "You take care, Billy Latham," he said. "We'll get word to you when we're settled someplace. Meantime, you just grow on up the way ye been growin', so's we can show young Billy Freeman what kind of man we mean for him to be."

He whipped up his team then, and off they went, down the dusty road. I stood there, looking after them — heart-broken, happy and proud. I watched till their wagon reached the top of the rise and disappeared down the other side.

And then I realized we'd never said good-bye.

EPILOGUE

Once, years afterward, a crumpled letter came to me from the hand of a Green Mountain man passing through on his way home from the War. The writing was faded, and the paper so crinkled that I could not make out all of the words. The gist of it was, Tom had been married to Sally by a Papist priest they met up with somewhere west of Pennsylvania. That same priest had written the letter, and he told how he had baptized a child born to Sally while they tarried there — a child called Billy Freeman.

Where Tom and Sally settled, I never learned. I guess now I will never know. But I like to think that Jordan knows, and is glad.

Poor little Billy Freeman, he never got to know his father. Nor did Charlie Ledyard. And both had such fathers as are given to very few. I think of them often, and when I do, I count myself among the fortunate of this earth. For I had such a father, and I have him still.

AUTHOR'S NOTE

BILLY LATHAM was lost at sea *circa* 1792.

The employees of THORNDIKE PRESS hope you have enjoyed this Large Print book. All our Large Print books are designed for easy reading — and they're made to last.

Other Thorndike Large Print books are available at your library, through selected bookstores, or directly from us. Suggestions for books you would like to see in Large Print are always welcome.

For more information about current and upcoming titles, please call or mail your name and address to:

THORNDIKE PRESS
PO Box 159
Thorndike, Maine 04986
800/223-6121
207/948-2962